OUR ENTANGLED FUTURE

EDITED BY

KAREN O'BRIEN
ANN EL KHOURY
NICOLE SCHAFENACKER
JORDAN ROSENFELD

This book was produced as part of the AdaptationCONNECTS research project, which is studying the relationship between climate change adaptation and transformations to sustainability. This 5-year project is funded by the Research Council of Norway (Project Number 250434/F10) and the University of Oslo.

O'Brien, K., El Khoury, A., Schafenacker, N. and Rosenfeld, J. (eds). 2019. *Our Entangled Future: Stories to Empower Quantum Social Change.* AdaptationCONNECTS Research Project, University of Oslo: Oslo, Norway.

Our Entangled Future can be downloaded free of charge from the following websites:
https://www.sv.uio.no/iss/english/research/projects/adaptation/news/our-entangled-future.htm
http://cchange.no/ourentangledfuture

ISBN (ePub): 978-82-691819-0-6
ISBN (pdf): 978-82-691819-2-0
ISBN (paperback): 978-82-691819-1-3

Cover: Michelle Fairbanks at Fresh Design
(mfairbanks.carbonmade.com)
Interior Design and Formatting: Qamber Design and Media
(qamberdesignsandmedia.com)

CONTENTS

IMAGES

PREFACE

Can we tell a new story about climate change? Can we use characters, imagery, and metaphors to communicate a sense of collective agency and reveal the potential that exists in every moment for social change? We thought it would be a good idea to try! This project came together because of a shared desire to bring potentiality to the forefront of our storytelling. We live our lives through stories, and if we want to create a thriving, sustainable world, we will need to change our story. We need narratives that convey our deepest values as humans and our greatest potential to respond collectively to climate change.

Our Entangled Future: Stories to Empower Quantum Social Change is part of the AdaptationCONNECTS research project, which is funded by the University of Oslo and the Research Council of Norway. AdaptationCONNECTS focuses on the relationship between adaptation and transformations to sustainability and explores the contributions of creativity, collaboration, empowerment, and new narratives. It also investigates the potential for new paradigms or thought patterns to shape the future, including those based on ideas drawn from quantum social science. The research engages with a growing recognition that to adapt successfully to climate change, we need to adapt to the very idea that we are creating the future right now. Adaptation is about transformation at the deepest levels, and there is no better way to transform than by telling new stories about ourselves and our significance in an entangled future. Could the use of new metaphors and images really contribute to a different narrative about climate change?

We announced a call for short stories related to the notion of "quantum social change," fully recognizing the ambiguity of the term. We wanted stories to explore a quantum paradigm, and were curious about the different ways that this would be interpreted. We deliberately pitched the call to both writers and researchers, in recognition that many of those who work daily with climate change are engaging with wider and deeper solution spaces. We sought stories that engage with a creative agility to reimagine the world from the perspective of a new paradigm.

The nine authors featured in *Our Entangled Future* responded with thoughtful, agency-driven characters and a revitalizing view of our world and the context in which we find ourselves. One of our favorite aspects of this collection is the global character of the stories. The writers or their work originate in Australia, Denmark, Germany, Mexico, the Netherlands, Pakistan, the Philippines, and South Africa. A development process for each text was also built into our project and we are grateful to writer and co-editor Jordan Rosenfeld for her careful hand in bringing forth what makes each narrative exceptional.

Three of the nine stories received jury awards for their innovation and excellence from our expert panel of Amy Brady, Adeline Johns-Putra and Rebecca Lawton. The award winning stories, *The Witnesses* by Chris Riedy, *The Drought* by Jessica Wilson, and *The Ephemeral Marvels Perfume Store* by Catherine Sarah Young provide three different interpretations of quantum social change. Interestingly, all of them take place in the future, yet draw attention to the potential we hold right now to generate transformative shifts. Partway through the project, we recognized the opportunity to feature compelling and evocative visual art, and we paired each story with an original image that relates to entanglement and the natural environment.

This book is a response to society's tepid progress on addressing the root causes of climate change. We consider these root causes to be fundamentally about how we see ourselves in the world, how we relate to each other and to the environment, and not the least, how we engage with the future. Writer and ecologist Robin Kimmerer speaks about writing as "an act of reciprocity with the world."[1] Reading too, can be a reciprocal, even a quantum, act. In fact, readers of these stories are participating in the unfolding possibilities described in this anthology. We hope you enjoy these nine stories and the accompanying art. Better yet – we hope that they inspire you to write your own story about quantum social change!

Karen O'Brien, Ann El Khoury, Nicole Schafenacker, and Jordan Rosenfeld
September 2019

---

1   Kimmerer 2013, p. 152.

I wanted to stay in that place, whatever it was.
© Elin Glærum Haugland, primusprimus.com

STORIES OF QUANTUM SOCIAL CHANGE

*by Karen O'Brien, Ann El Khoury, Nicole Schafenacker
and Jordan Rosenfeld*

> *"New metaphors have the power to create a new reality."*
> (Lakoff and Johnson, 1980, p. 145)

1. INTRODUCTION

Anyone who reads the news these days will recognize that climate change is anything but fiction. Real stories of risk, danger, and loss are conveyed to us daily, whether in relation to wildfires, floods, droughts, heatwaves, glacial melting, rising waters, coral bleaching, species losses, or any other type of ecological distress. The protagonists in these stories are many – they include firefighters, farmers, coastal communities, elected officials, scientists, activists, governments, and those of us who have a stake in maintaining a planet that is hospitable to life. The protagonists in climate change are not merely observers; they are also taking action, for a good story always includes action. Our protagonists are marching in the streets, running for public office, standing up in the boardroom, directing theater pieces, organizing meetings and festivals, and introducing alternatives to our energy-intensive, consumer-oriented lifestyles.

The antagonists in today's climate stories are numerous as well, including the oil industry, capitalism, agribusinesses, mining interests, mass tourism, and "people like us" who have adapted to paradigms of perpetual progress, endless consumption, unlimited growth, or the idea that "technology will save us." The story of climate change is often told as a heroic battle of good versus evil, right versus wrong, and us versus them. As this plot unfolds, many people are starting to look more closely at the narratives underlying the story of climate change. What kind of stories are we actually telling ourselves and each other about our future in a changing climate? More importantly, what messages are we conveying about our potential to influence the future, right here and now?

Stories play a powerful role in transmitting personal and collective experiences. They allow us to "feel" climate change in ways that can move us emotionally and open our imagination to new possibilities. They raise our awareness not only to what is happening in the world, but to how it may be experienced by others, both now and in the future. In doing this, stories can change our world. Indeed, the climate crisis requires us to imagine other ways of living—a task to which, of all cultural forms, fiction is the most suited. As Amitav Ghosh writes in *The Great Derangement*, "let us make no mistake: the climate crisis is also a crisis of culture, and thus of the imagination."[1]

Climate fiction, or "cli-fi," is a literary genre that is rapidly expanding in response to the climate crisis, with new books and anthologies coming out every day. Cli-fi is located within a broader genre of speculative or science fiction. Speculative fiction is particularly well suited to addressing the climate crisis, as it can activate both reflection and engagement and thus serve as an effective vehicle for expressing experiential impacts, social criticism and alternative scenarios. Speculative fiction can also be used to develop strategic thought experiments related to both practical and philosophical ideas. As an art-science form, it has a unique capacity to envision possible, probable, and preferred collective futures based on projections of available scientific data. It can also draw attention to the importance of consciousness, subjectivity, agency and lived experiences of the climate crisis. It demonstrates humanity's complex co-implication with the natural world in a more subjective and emotional way. Speculative fiction has the potential to help us to recognize our own potential in co-creating the future. This potential has not yet been fully activated.

---

1   Ghosh 2016, p. 9

Much of contemporary climate fiction depicts a dystopic world that has been radically transformed by the impacts of climate change. For example, in the introduction to *Change Everything: An Anthology of Climate Fiction*, Manjana Milkoreit and her coeditors write that "most of our stories imagine gloomy, dystopian future worlds in which much of what we cherish – and take for granted – about our present realities will be lost."[2] In the Foreword to *Loosed Upon the World: The Saga Anthology of Climate Fiction*, editor John Joseph Adams describes the stories as a warning flare "to illustrate the kinds of things we can expect if climate change goes unchecked." However, he also suggests that they may reveal some possible solutions that "inspire the hope that we can maybe still do something about it before it's too late…"[3] This is critical at a time when many are giving up hope on the future.

Stories have to offer us more than hope. They have to help us to imagine *and* actualize alternative "not-yet-here" realities that enable people and our planet to thrive. They can encourage us to question dominant modes of thinking, relating, acting, and governing, and they can inspire new understandings of the patterns and relationships that are shaping our future. Speculative fiction offers the opportunity to activate thought patterns that empower us with agency and leave us knowing that we can collectively create a better future. They can help us perceive, feel, and activate the possibilities for social change.

As Ernest Callenbach, author of the 1970s classic, *Ecotopia*, said in an interview: "It is so hard to imagine anything fundamentally different from what we have now. But without these alternate visions, we get stuck on dead center. And we'd better get ready. We need to know where we'd like to go."[4] Callenbach's *Ecotopia* was a forerunner to an eco-future movement of practical utopianism known as solarpunk. In contrast to the darkness of popular apocalyptic science fiction, solarpunk offers more viable, optimistic stories about the near-futures and coping with the climate crisis, with the goal of encouraging and inspiring people to change the present. Recognizing that political, social and cultural shifts will be necessary for

---

2   Milkoreit 2016, p. xvi.
3   Adams 2015, p. xii
4   Cited in Timberg 2008.

more sustainable futures, it deploys radical optimism to bring greener futures into being. It is at once a countercultural movement, an adaptation art form, and "a form of futurism that focuses on what we should hope for rather than on what to avoid."[5] Its themes are thrivability and generativity. At its best, propositional speculative fiction and solarpunk can function as a realism of the possible, helping us think through the world as it is and as it may be.

The full realm of possibilities for social change is not likely to be realized through a mechanistic Newtonian paradigm. This scientific paradigm emerged during the 18th century Age of Enlightenment, also known as the "Age of Reason." Among other things, it distinguishes subjects from objects; views space and time as absolute; sees individuals as separate and discrete; includes a limited role for free will and consciousness; and considers causality to be deterministic. This is indeed a problem, for if humans are responsible for climate change and environmental degradation, our lack of conscious agency and real connection make it unlikely that we will transform systems at the rate and scale that is called for at this time. Quantum social change suggests that there may be other ways to understand and generate transformations to sustainability.

2. Quantum Social Change

What do we mean by "quantum social change"? Quantum social change describes a nonlinear, non-local approach to sustainability transformations. This approach recognizes that our deepest values and intentions are the source of individual change, collective change, *and* systems change. Drawing on metaphors from quantum physics, and referencing the ambiguous interpretations of its fundamental meaning, quantum social change recognizes the potential for transformations through concepts borrowed from quantum physics, such as entanglement, the wave-particle duality, complementarity, superposition and not the least, by generating a metaphorical "quantum leap." This leap, which can be considered a transition that is sudden or discrete (i.e., without intermediate stages), calls for us to activate a new paradigm, right here and now.

---

5   Solarpunk Anarchists n.d.

There are many popular science books describing the history and significance of quantum physics, including its strange implications for our understanding of reality. For example, Philip Ball's *Beyond Weird: Why Everything You Thought You Knew About Quantum Physics is Different* emphasizes that the most fundamental message of quantum theory is not a mathematical one, it is about words. Language, he argues, "is the only vehicle we have for constructing and conveying meaning: for talking about our universe."[6] This is precisely why new stories are so important. Without a scientific consensus on the fundamental nature of reality, it is up to us to develop a language for describing what is possible. Indeed, some interpretations of quantum physics suggest that we are, in fact, responsible for writing the script. Yet we also live in a world of classical physics, where the molecules of carbon dioxide released through the burning of fossil fuels heat the atmosphere; where ice melts at certain temperatures; and where physical changes have profound implications for the totality of the social and natural world. The understanding that humans play an important role in the Earth system draws attention to the need for social change. The recognition that the human-environment duality is just a cultural story suggests that it may be time to explore the story of quantum social change.

Why quantum social change? We need stories that confront the limitations of a dualistic, deterministic, and inanimate worldview and instead offer insights into a reality that is connected, entangled, uncertain, and ripe with possibility – a world of complementarity, non-locality, and potentiality. In *Reality is Not What it Seems*, physicist Carlo Rovelli reminds us that "[t]he world is more extraordinary and profound than any of the fables told by our forefathers."[7] Or as physicist and feminist scholar Karen Barad writes, "[t]he world and its possibilities for becoming are remade with each moment."[8] The idea of "quantum social change" may, at the very least, serve as a powerful metaphor to activate individual and collective agency for generating social change.

------

6   Ball 2018, p. 346.
7   Rovelli 2016, p. 233.
8   Barad 2007, p. 196.

3. Stories to Empower Quantum Social Change

Can we strategically evoke fictional narratives of quantum social change in the service of transformations to a sustainable and thriving world? As mentioned above, to date most cli-fi has communicated depleting and diminishing apocalyptic imaginaries. Cautionary narratives have their place, but we need aspirational tales of successful social change and systems change, for they too can be a reality. The role of narratives and imaginaries can be seen as akin to fractals or self-similar patterns that replicate at all scales, opening up new possibilities and potentials for change. The fractal space of narratives holds boundless potential. As fractals, we build the future one idea and action at a time.

New narrative arcs, images and metaphors allow us to imagine a possible trajectory for the story of our time and our individual roles in weaving this future. Through story, interconnections are revealed allowing us to foster new partnerships between each other and the world we inhabit, and to participate in the world that is becoming. Activist and writer Joanna Macy inquires into this process using systems theory. She adopts Ervin Laszlo's term "exploratory self-organization" to describe the courageous act of engaging the middle-space where one releases old patterning but does not yet know how the new pattern looks, or how the story ends, so to speak.[9] Fictional narratives are waves of potential in world-making. Readers and writers are entangled in acts of meaning-making; stories are at once individual and collective cultural acts.

Philosophically, a quantum-influenced realism points out that what is "not yet," or "in potentia" is actually part of reality. Speculative fiction invites us to embrace the wave-particle duality as the space of potential between the writer and the reader, and the imagined and the actual. Metaphorically, it highlights how people are at once both the problem and the solution in the climate crisis. As one of our jurors, Adeline Johns-Putra writes in response to the anthology, "Climate change and other components of the Anthropocene disclose a disturbing paradox: human agency bears at once blame and responsibility. It must therefore be simultaneously de-centred

---

9   Macy 1998, p.45.

(to acknowledge that we are not exceptional from other species) and re-centred (to acknowledge our ethical obligations to these species)."

4. THE STORIES

The nine stories that make up *Our Entangled Future* represent diverse interpretations of quantum social change. The call for short stories was left quite open, as we were aware of the challenges of imagining what a quantum paradigm has to offer. We asked each author to describe how they interpreted quantum social change within their story, and we have paired each story with a piece of visual art. Based on an evaluation by our jury, three stories were recognized as notable. Below, we present a short summary of each of these stories, reflecting on how we as editors relate them to the idea of an entangled future that is empowered through quantum social change.

In *The Witnesses*, Chris Riedy looks at both the dark and light sides of entanglement. His story starts from the current world, where people have tuned out of reality and engage as voyeurs in a virtual reality. The narrator tells an honest story of a personal and collective journey of awakening, starting with an awareness that "even in the comfort of the virtual, many of us had a nagging feeling that something was missing." Triggered by a high-tech witnessing of a family drowning in Bangladeshi floods, it is a story of searching, connecting, realizing, and acting. *The Witnesses* highlights the importance of holding a bigger and more coherent strategy for social change. The transformation that results is gradual and intangible, yet leads to a collective recognition of the power of seeking well-being through connections with others. Importantly, it is not a firm victory – the process of regenerating the Earth takes time. Yet the motivation that drives people to change in this story is an important one: It is the search for meaning and realization that "there is always still work to be done." As Riedy's story shows, the more opportunities we have to bear witness to each other's narratives, the greater the potential for building our compassion and for using our collective knowledge for quantum social change.

In *The Drought*, Jessica Wilson helps us to imagine an expansion of our human capacity to the point that we no longer feel disconnected and instead operate as one organism, a theme addressed by several of our authors. *The Drought* begins with a story within a story of how it all started ("Time wraps in on itself") and the crisis that led to the transformation: "Whether it happened in a moment or over centuries, no one could say. But everyone agreed that when the seas rose to their maximum height and the earth reached its hottest temperatures, things were different. The human species changed." Wilson describes the transition from a classical reality to a quantum reality. In the classical world, people "had disconnected their thoughts from their feelings, themselves from each other, their species from the web-of-life and their souls from the sacred. And they had projected this peculiar and sad form of reality onto a self-aware, living cosmos, of which they were a part." In the quantum world, "people were still individuals at the same time that they were part of a larger whole." The main characters, Sylvia and her granddaughter, Karipi, are entangled within this new world. Through Karipi, we are invited to wonder, to wrestle, and to make sense of our own shadows in relationship to a planet in need of healing. Can the tightly-wound knots that distance us from the world and each other be transmuted into agency? Karipi turns to the interconnections between the mind/body and the natural world for knowledge to bring herself to the other side of complex questions related to the healing of both individual and collective trauma.

Stories, including the story of our time, often come into being precisely because of conflict. Quantum social change is *not* about utopian futures. It recognizes that things that we value will be lost, and that adaptation to climate change will continue to be a necessary part of the future. In *The Ephemeral Marvels Perfume Store*, Catherine Sarah Young tells the story about scents from the natural world that we may not be able to experience in the future -- something that is rarely considered when discussing the impacts of climate change. Her story follows Emilia, a perfumer living on a floating city who makes concoctions from plants that have all but disappeared from the Earth. Young's story is about the power of smell to evoke memories from earlier times: "Older people wanted to recall the memories of their youth when there was much more to smell, such as the scents of older varieties of fruits and flowers, and the odors of seasons when they were more distinct. Younger ones wanted new experiences, though

Emilia was saddened that they would never get to smell a field of lavender or a beach with coconut trees." Interestingly, some biologists regard our sense of smell to be a quantum phenomenon. In *Life on the Edge: The Coming of Age of Quantum Biology*, Jim Al-Khalili and Johnjoe McFadden explore the nature of smell, pointing out just how remarkable the olfactory sense is and how poorly understood it remains. A quantum theory of scent points to the role of vibration and the quantum mechanism of electron tunneling in the functioning of olfactory receptors.[10] The olfactory experiments carried out by Emilia show that this is indeed a remarkable sense, in that our nose is closely linked to memory: "If she faced all of her perfumes, she could distinguish each of them and remember the occasion for which it was mixed. Her perfumes were like dear companions in these lonely times of uncertainty and loss."

Each of the stories introduce a unique perspective on quantum social change. Juror Amy Brady writes that within these stories, "[t]he characters entangled with each other and their landscapes [are] true models of compassion and empathy," and that, "[t]he metaphors emphasize connectedness and uncertainty." We see that are there are endless ways to approach change, and that it may be more mysterious, more irreverent, or even more ordinary than we think. In *The Legend of the Cosmos Mariners*, Kelli Rose Pearson's allegorical tale about caring for the Earth, the quirky character Aunt Bloom relays this in response to young Zella's question about how to become a Cosmos Mariner: "Well, there are many, many ways. As many ways are there are heartbeats." Nature, too, is explored as having agency. In *The Green Lizard* by Albert van Wijngaarden, the character Manu finds comfort in a nocturnal encounter with a shape-shifting green lizard as he untangles the conflicting views of his community on a conservation initiative. Manu wonders, "Maybe not all was lost. Nature grows and lives inside houses too. Maybe it can adjust, adapt, and grow again?"

In the same way that Young draws on sense of smell in *The Ephemeral Marvels Perfume Store*, several authors explore the ways our bodies and senses give way to deep knowing and interconnection with our world

---

10   McFadden and Al Khalili 2014.

through taste, touch and sound. In *The Green Lizard,* Ajith "reached up with his right arm and clanged the bell. The clear sound broke the silence in the temple and in his heart." The question of how to transmute, or alchemically recycle, our darker human experiences into something useful is also considered. In Saher Hasnain's *Let Us Begin,* the character Amreen speaks about deep attunement to the environment as a beginning point for knowledge of quantum reality. She gets there through the experience of a daily and ancient injustice: "Women in our country have always been viscerally aware of their surroundings. Far more aware than men have had to be. We can *feel* eyes on us... My sister and I wondered how we could use this visceral awareness." Otter Lieffe's *Synergy* takes us beyond our human senses and ask us to imagine being able to taste the blending of waters from different streams as a perch, or to sense the night's echoes through the tiny hairs on a moth, or pipistrelle's, body. These stories suggest that we are entangled through our senses, experiences, and consciousness.

Both Julia Naime Sánchez-Henkel's *The Visitor* and Jude Anderson's *Cool Burn and the Cherry Ballart* draw attention to the importance of Indigenous knowledges and of times where humans not only co-existed with their natural environments, but lived in mutually beneficial ways with other species. In *The Visitor,* Naime Sánchez-Henkel's character of Manshika, the *Shihuahuaco* tree, muses on human mutability and skill: "Humans impressed me because they had all types of animals inside them." Jude Anderson and her collaborator, Ado, or Adrian Webster, go into the heart of colonial history on the banks of the Bangalee River, using the content and form of *Cool Burn and The Cherry Ballart* to recognize that we cannot untangle climate change without simultaneously uprooting colonialization. Much of this story is driven by deep listening. Ado invites the guests of his Country into a view of deep interconnection: "My people, our story, Wandi Wandian clan, how we connect to country, respect it, our law, our language, creation stories, it's all one. We learn here on Country."

In small, seemingly innocuous, instances we may recognize in these stories the human edges of our vulnerability: "Every human craves connection. They show this with their hundreds of online friendships and desires for validation from people they've never met," quips Sameena in *Let Us Begin.* Each author asks us to consider and to participate in the in-between space of writer to reader, of thought to action, in the swampy middle ground of not knowing, for in this there is potential. As Aunt Bloom tells the children, "Don't forget, my dears – the universe is not only stranger than we imagine, it's stranger than we CAN imagine!" She also reminds us that "Everything touches everything in a big, chaotic tangle of tangledness. This means that every small act of kindness ripples out and touches everything else." In Otter Lieffe's *Synergy*, we experience through the main character Maria that "no matter how much things changed, no matter how much their lives were disrupted, some cycles continued. She turned her back on the city and, smiling for no good reason, stepped back inside to start again."

Starting again is a practice, and it takes practice. Aunt Bloom reminds us that "[i]t takes practice to see through the eyes of a river, an ant, or another person." In *The Witnesses*, Riedy's character captures the challenges associated with this practice: "Growing your compassion for the distant other is a slow and painful transformation, with steps forward and steps backward. It's messy." In *Let Us Begin*, Hasnain describes the power of practice: "This is the brink of something wonderful. You have experienced how natural our connection feels. And, it will get deeper and more meaningful, the more we do it." As Naime Sánchez-Henkel puts it in *The Visitor*, "Nature becomes fantastical when you give yourself the time to explore it. Attention, properly applied to anything, will reveal you marvels."

5. CONCLUSION

We need new stories of change, and the collection presented in this anthology represents some of the many ways of relating to "Our Entangled Future." In a recently published article in *The Outline*, Siobhan Leddy references the work of the late Ursula LeGuin as an example of the kind of story our time requires: "The kind of story we need right now is unheroic, incorporating social movements, political imagination and nonhuman actors."[11] Likewise, Adeline Johns-Putra notes that, "Our stories may occur as an intra-species activity (conveyed, related, shared amongst humans), but they must communicate a wider inter-species consciousness (addressing, redressing, and even reversing the damage

---

11   Leddy 2019.

that we have inflicted on our planetary fellows and on the biosphere as a whole)." Many of the stories presented here weave the imagined realities of nonhuman actors into narrative tapestries that convey the wonders already cycling around us humans. As well, many draw on these wondrous natural entities for wisdom and resilience. Perhaps we are called to be like the fynbos in Jessica Wilson's story, *The Drought*: "Used to endless cycles of drought and fire, the plants making up the richest floral kingdom in the world continued to breathe and blossom."

It may be that one of our deepest resources, in tandem with our imaginings of wider and deeper solution spaces to address climate change, is our ability to remain connected to one another and our world. For we are always entangled in a world that we are collectively co-creating. As Rebecca Lawton writes, "Only in imagining where our current trajectory takes us, from perspectives as wide and deeply creative as those shared by the authors here, does a different future become possible." Our vision is that these stories will evoke your own intimate and deep connections to the ways you/we relate to the world. We hope that they activate your imagination, inspire connections, and awaken a sense of belonging in this world as we collectively transform it by bringing together tenderness of heart, embodied listening, and conscious action. It is time to generate quantum social change.

References

Adams, John Joseph (ed). 2015. *Loosed Upon the World: The Saga Anthology of Climate Fiction*. New York: Saga Press.

Al-Khalili, Jim and McFadden, Johnjoe. 2014. *Life on the Edge: The Coming of Age of Quantum Biology.* London: Bantam Books.

Ball, Philip. 2019. *Beyond Weird: Why Everything You Thought You Knew About Quantum Physics is Different*. London: Vintage.

Barad, Karen. 2007. *Meeting the Universe Halfway: Quantum Physics and the Entanglement of Matter and Meaning.* Durham: Duke University Press.

Callenbach, Ernest. 1975 (1990). *Ecotopia: The Notebooks and Reports of William Weston*. New York: Bantam.

Ghosh, Amitav 2016. *The Great Derangement: Climate Change and the Unthinkable*. Chicago: University of Chicago Press.

Kimmerer, Robin Wall. 2013. *Braiding Sweetgrass: Indigenous Wisdom, Scientific Knowledge and the Teachings of Plants*. Minneapolis: Milkweed Editions.

Lakoff, G. and Johnson, M. 1980. *Metaphors We Live By*. Chicago: University of Chicago Press.

Leddy, Siobhan. 2019. 'We should all be reading more Ursula Le Guin', The Outline, Aug 28, URL: https://theoutline.com/post/7886/ursula-leguin-carrier-bag-theory

Macy, J. & Brown, M. Y. 1998. *Coming back to life: Practices to reconnect our lives, our world*. Gabriola Island, BC: New Society Publishers.

Milkoreit, M, Martinez, M and Eschrich, J (eds.). 2016. *Everything Change: An Anthology of Climate Fiction*. Tempe, Arizona: Arizona State University.

Rovelli, Carlo. 2016. *Reality Is Not What It Seems: The Journey to Quantum Gravity*. Penguin Books.

Solarpunk Anarchist, n. d. About, https://solarpunkanarchists.com/about/

Timberg, Scott. 2008. 'The Novel that Predicted Portland', *New York Times*, https://www.nytimes.com/2008/12/14/fashion/14ecotopia.html

Light Waves by © Tone Bjordam, tonebjordam.com

The Witnesses

by Chris Riedy

But speak the truth, and all nature and all spirits help you with unexpected furtherance. Speak the truth, and all things alive or brute are vouchers, and the very roots of the grass underground there, do seem to stir and move to bear you witness.
— Ralph Waldo Emerson, Divinity School Address, 1838

We weren't trying to save the world. Not at the start anyway. I wish I could say our motives were always pure, but the truth is more complicated, messier, harder to pin down.

We did care. The world was burning around us, roasting in its own excess. The airwaves were saturated with a jarring mix of disaster and hedonism – extreme deprivation and obscene wealth. Media was everywhere, but meaning was elusive. We knew something had to change but we had no idea how our actions could make any difference. The world was charging off a cliff with eight billion souls on board.

Politics had turned into a circus—there was no salvation there. Corporations were mostly psychopaths, focused on tearing profit out of the Earth as fast as they could, with no thought for the future. Movements came and went but none of them built lasting power.

To top it all off, there was no sense of urgency. We experienced climate change as a slow-motion disaster that seemed to hurt people far away from us in time and space—future generations or the poor global masses. Doom crept up behind us but our wealth cushioned us from the worst impacts.

And so, I'm sorry to say, we tuned out. It all seemed too hard and too far away, so we escaped into our screens, our shopping, our addictions, our socials, our splintered tribes. We tried to shut out our desperate and meaningless reality by retreating into other worlds. Those worlds became increasingly real and immersive, far more compelling and meaningful than the crumbling civilisation around us. This made things worse, of course. We spent more and more time in the virtual and paid less and less attention to the truths written in the unravelling of ecosystems and the screams of refugees.

Yet, even in the comfort of the virtual, many of us had a nagging sense that something was missing. In the virtual, nothing real was on the line. We knew that, deep down. In the virtual, we were heroes and gods, but when we took off our sets, the real world came rushing back. The contrast was jarring. We stepped out onto a treadmill of working and shopping and posing and fighting for space on a crowded planet. Our mental health suffered, as we struggled to bridge the disconnect between the real and the virtual, to find some way to align those very different worlds. That's how it started. We were looking for something real in the virtual. It's not a nice story, but bear with me—it ends well.

I crouched in the corner of a tiny, cramped room, mud under my bare feet, a tin wall rattling at my back. A woman and four children huddled with me, terror shining in their eyes, their bright clothing soaked through and blotched with filth. The noise was visceral, a howling wind and pounding rain that shook our cramped shelter. The tin roof jumped and clanged back into place, then, with a great tearing sound, it lifted away. The din intensified and rain pounded my skin. I crawled through the mud toward the door but before I could get there it burst open and a torrent of brown debris-filled water rushed in. The force knocked me into a corner. I tried to get to my feet but could make no headway against the powerful flow. I reached for the others and clung to them as the room filled and my vision blurred. I pounded the wall with desperation once, twice but it made no impression. Distorted by the water now filling the room, I looked into the face of a little girl as she opened her mouth in search of air and gulped filthy water instead. I opened my own mouth to scream, the world tilted as the wall behind me collapsed and my vision faded into black.

I tore off my set and light flooded back in, illuminating the familiar surroundings of my room.

"What the hell was that? It felt so real," I said.

"It was real. You just died, mate." Jed's voice floated over my shoulder from behind me.

"What do you mean?" I said, turning to face him.

"It's the latest thing," he said. "It's called a *scene*. They pay some poor schmuck in Bangladesh or somewhere a few bucks to have a V-cam implanted that uploads the footage."

"Seriously? Who'd agree to something like that?" I thought maybe he was winding me up.

"You'd be surprised, mate. Life's tough over there. The surgery is really simple, no big risk. And the money can make all the difference when you've got a family to feed. Heaps of people have gone for it. They give up a bit of privacy to survive."

"Of course," Jed continued, "most of the footage is rubbish. Life in the Third World isn't exactly riveting entertainment. But when something big happens, like those Bangladeshi floods or a resource war, they comb through the footage, pull out the best stuff and sell it to rich kids like us who're looking for a thrill."

"No way! Are people really that desperate?" Another thought occurred to me: "Who's *they?*"

"I dunno, but it's all over the dark web. Not just storms and floods either. There's all sorts of bad shit from the Third World," Jed said. "They must be raking it in for that one though—have you ever felt anything like it?"

"Never. Don't you think it's kind of sick though? They're living off the misery of those poor people."

Jed was unmoved. "Sure, but it's not like they're being forced to do it. It's a good deal for the cammers if they survive, and if they're dead, what do they care who sees the footage? Check out this site if you want to see more. But be careful. That one was pretty tame compared to some of the stuff out there."

Images of children's faces, distorted by muddy water, haunted my sleep that night. In the morning, I took to the web to find out more about what I had seen. Everything I could find indicated it was genuine footage from the recent Bangladesh floods. I'd heard about them in the news—tens of thousands dead, millions displaced—but in a sea of bad news those numbers had meant little to me. Somehow it was different now. Those numbers had faces, families. Each was a moment of horror followed by blackness.

I struggled with my conscience for a while. Did I really want to be a voyeur into these broken lives? But the *scene* had moved something in me like nothing else had in a long time. It was a shocking glimpse of reality, so foreign from my sheltered world.

I didn't feel good about it, but I went looking for more.

The sun was bright, so bright. I was in some kind of desert landscape, trudging in a line of emaciated, ragged-looking women. The earth beneath my feet was parched and cracked. The world around me was yellow and brown, no green to be seen. I held my arms up, as if to steady an object on my head, but it was out of sight. Other women in the line were balancing large clay pots on their heads. The line shuffled forward and, ahead, a crowd gathered around something hidden from view. Our line foundered as it met the seething mass of people and I was quickly surrounded by a press of bodies, all pushing towards the centre of the circle. People were shouting, voices raised in anger and fear. A woman near me stumbled, her pot crashed to the ground, and she was quickly swallowed by the crowd. A gap opened ahead of me for a moment and I squeezed into it, catching a glimpse of the object at the centre of the crowd—a water pump. A great shout rose up from the crowd, rippling outwards. I didn't understand the words but they sent us all into a frenzy. The crowd became a mob, dissolving into chaos, all pushing towards the centre. I fell, my vision dipping suddenly and sickeningly toward the ground, and the pot I was carrying crashed and shattered in front of me. A dizzying blur of feet surrounded me, pressing in on all sides. Once again, briefly, I had a clear line of sight to the water pump. A woman pumped the handle frantically, but nothing flowed from the tap. Then the feet pressed in again and my vision faded to black.

Scenes used brand new technology, hacked from what the big corporations put out. Devices had got so tiny they could be implanted with minimal risk to the host. We weren't at the point where you could tap into what people were actually seeing or feeling but you could implant cameras beside their eyes and mics by their ears and with some fancy software you could stream video and audio that was hard to distinguish from reality. Even in our social media world, not many people in the rich countries and enclaves were willing to share their lives to that extent. But in the poor majority world, just as Jed had said, there were plenty of people who would endure the inconvenience to put food on the table.

In the early days, the *sceners* were ambulance chasers. They waited for news of a disaster or conflict and then combed through footage from anyone in the area who was cammed up to find the most compelling and dramatic moments, to be sold on the dark web. Later, they developed software algorithms that could process vast quantities of footage to find the drama in the mundane. The *scenes* became more sophisticated and the *sceners* got better at telling stories. It was a sick little industry, a product of our times, pandering to rich kids who wanted to experience something real in a manufactured world.

For me, it became an addiction, for a while. I hunted down these moments of horror driven by a morbid fascination and a sense that here, at last, was something real in the din of the virtual and hedonistic. Sometimes I felt dirty, but there was a weird purity to it as well. As if I was bearing witness to these lives cut short, giving them a dignity that climate disaster had taken from them. I know that doesn't make much sense. It was a messed-up time for me. It felt like the world was crumbling around me and there was no meaning to be found in my life, so I looked for it in these other lives.

I wasn't the only one. It didn't take long before I hooked up with others who had gone down this path. There is always a tribe to be found these days—there's so many of us on the planet now, and we're so connected. Ours was a dark web community, under the radar of popular media. The implanted V-kits used to record the *scenes* were illegal so we were engaged in something illicit. I have to admit, that added to the thrill. Despite the danger, the risk of discovery, we still found each other. We linked up, we shared *scenes*, we talked. Some of those conversations, tentatively, awkwardly, started to touch on what we could do for the people whose lives we were spying on. How could we move from powerless voyeurs to something more? And some of the *sceners* started to tell different kinds of stories.

I am surrounded by blue light streaming down in rays from above, bubbles rising around me. I am suspended above a rich tapestry of life, a coral reef, teeming with colourful, tropical fish. I move slowly forward and can see my hands reaching out, pulling water, propelling me. The scene is one of great abundance. Hard and soft corals of many kinds stretch as far as I can see, tiny fish dart in and out amongst them, and larger silver fish pass by in dense schools. Then—a moment of total darkness before the blue light rushes back in. Jarringly, the scene is utterly changed. I am in the same place—I can recognise a distinctive rocky outcrop that I had been looking at. But the colour is gone. The corals have become white skeletons. Where there were schools of fish are now only drifting clouds of pale jellyfish. With another dizzying transition, I am sitting in a boat, alone on a blue sea. My brown, calloused hands are in front of me, pulling on a rope that runs over the side of the boat. I heave on the rope until a net emerges from the depths. I lift it into the boat, loosen the rope encircling the mouth of the net and pull it open. A few gelatinous bodies—jellyfish —are all that the net contains. My hands rise to my face in a movement of despair and the scene fades to black.

You probably think I'm going to say I had an awakening, an epiphany, a sudden moment of clarity. I didn't. It's not that simple. I wish it were, but it's not. Growing your compassion for the distant other is a slow and painful transformation, with steps forward and steps backward. It's messy. I started in a pretty dark place, with no sense that I could have any impact on the world around me, but even so, I know I was already changing when I experienced that flood in Bangladesh. I was already searching for something. That first *scene* was an important marker on my journey. I started, slowly, to care about people I knew nothing about, far from my life. A seed was planted in my mind that grew and grew. But along the way there was no moment of clarity, just a sense of wrongness about my life that drove me to search and strive to make it right. I still shopped, drove, drank, did all those things that made me part of the problem. But I started to make changes, make connections, expand my circle of care until I was part of something bigger, and there, I eventually found meaning.

I'd been to Kho Pha-Ngan before. I'd done the Full Moon Party, done the drugs, done the scene. I'd blogged about it, enthusiastically. But this time, I felt hollow. I couldn't connect to the thumping beat, the pulsing crowd, the dancers with their glazed eyes and fixed smiles. I wandered, aimlessly, towards the beach and found my way out onto a rickety pier.

A voice from the darkness startled me: "Why you out here?" The red glow of a cigarette illuminated the wrinkled face of an old man for a moment. "Party that way" he added, gesturing with his cigarette.

"I know. I just needed some air." I squinted into the darkness, tried to make out his face.

"Plenty air out here. You sit?" The glowing tip of his cigarette waved towards the pier edge, beside him.

I sat. It felt like the right thing to do. We were both silent for a moment, then he said "I used to fish here. Many years ago now. There were many fish for my family. Now, fish are gone. Only Farang come here now."

I glanced at him. There was no rebuke in his voice, just a weary resignation. We talked for a while. He told me a little of his life, his family, his beloved island, the changes he had lived through, his fears for the future. Mostly, I listened. My stories, from a life of privilege, seemed insubstantial compared to his. As he spoke, I could feel an unfocused pain growing in me, for all that he had lost—for all that *we* had lost. Then he finished his last cigarette and went on his way. I sat on the pier until light seeped into the sky, seeking some answer to the pain.

We called ourselves the Witnesses. There were four of us—Rohit, Cassie, Aamira and me. I was a pro blogger. I wrote, I recorded, I cast, and I lived off hits and ad revenue. A few years back, I would have been called a journalist, but the walls between corporate and social media had come down and anyone could write or cast for a living now, if they were good enough. I was good enough, although money was usually tight. I wrote travel pieces mainly, working my way around the world searching for new experiences, new angles that would get me enough views to keep moving. I had a good following and my first tentative attempts to write about the impacts of climate change viewed well, so I kept on going. I didn't mention *scenes* explicitly—they were illegal after all—but I wrote about those borrowed experiences as if I had been there and a lot of people seemed to connect with these tangible stories of the havoc wreaked by climate change. Then, I met Cassie.

I am making my way through an immense hall filled with stalls, exhibits, entertainers and throngs of people. The big screens flash "Regen10:

Technology to regenerate the Earth." These Regen conferences began as a side event alongside the annual UN climate change conferences, but now, they feel like the main game. They're a showcase for world-changing technologies. I meander between exhibits about new solar film technologies, self-recharging wearables, fast-growing trees, lab-grown carbon-neutral meat and automated electric cars, pausing to chat with some of the exhibitors and hear their crowdfunding pitches. They are all trying to save the world in their own way, and regenerate the damage we've already done.

In the centre of the exhibition hall there is a crowded bar. I grab a seat at the bar, just vacated by a tall Indian youth whose t-shirt is emblazoned with a single staring eye. I order an over-priced organic beer and settle back to look at the big screen above. Traditionally, Regen conferences provide a focal point for colourful climate change protests, but this one has turned violent. The footage shows a striking dark-skinned woman being dragged away by police. She's screaming at the camera: "You call this a crime! Climate change is the real crime. My people are dying while you talk in circles and play with your toys." I shake my head.

"You disagree?" The question comes from a woman beside me, blonde, well-dressed in eco-chic, North American from her accent. She looks at me with an unsettling intensity.

"No, it's not that," I say. "She should be angry. I'm angry too. I just don't think we're going to win most people over with that kind of argument. And the violence makes climate change look like an issue for extremists, not the mainstream."

"I completely agree. There's no strategy to what she's doing." She smiles and extends her hand. "I'm Cassie by the way."

She tells me she's Canadian, a consumer psychology and marketing expert. She worked for big corporations early in her career, learning how to sell anything to anyone. She took a job at Tesla, not because she cared about the planet, but because "it was cool." She rolls her eyes as she says it. That job changed her—or rather, the people she worked with and their passion for change really got to her. She started to question her purpose and it wasn't long before even Tesla felt like part of the problem.

"I felt like we were just selling toys to rich kids and we weren't ready to step up and tackle big problems like poverty and climate change," she says. "There wasn't much market in selling renewables to the developing world so we didn't try. I got out, floated through a bunch of social marketing roles in the NGO world and wound up working with EarthTech. They're not perfect, but at least they're tackling the real problems and trying to repair the damage we've all done."

She pauses, looks thoughtful and meets my eye again with that same strange intensity.

"You're right you know," she says. "Anger is important. Protest is important. But it needs to be one tactic in a much bigger strategy."

We talked into the night, and the idea for the Witnesses was born there, at an unremarkable bar, scribbled on a coaster.

Aamira's story is more mysterious. She was the woman on the screen, whose righteous anger inspired Cassie and me to connect. Cassie reached out to her through socials after Regen10. They had a heated argument about tactics that rolled on for several weeks, before they came to an understanding and started to strategise together. But even when she was part of the Witnesses, she didn't share much and didn't like to talk about her past. We knew she was Sudanese-born and that she had lost family in the Pan-Africa Famine. No doubt, that fuelled her anger and militance. She was connected into activist and civil disobedience networks and perhaps some shadier groups. If we needed something done, she knew a way to make it happen. More importantly, she was our conscience, the voice of the climate refugees. Any time the Witnesses started to feel like a game for rich kids, she would remind us what was at stake, and not gently.

Which just leaves Rohit. A Bangalorian hacker. He'd made a lot of money developing apps for the booming Indian market but his heroes were people like Julian Assange and Anonymous—hackers who turned over rocks and shone a light on what was crawling underneath. His dark web contacts introduced him to *scenes* when they first popped up and one from rural India really got under his skin. It sent him off on a pilgrimage into the heartland of his own country, part spiritual awakening, part bearing witness to the horrors of climate change. India has all the extremes that the rest of the planet has within the boundaries of one nation, and Rohit witnessed them firsthand. He toured the villages of Tamil Nadu after the monsoon failed and saw families dying of thirst, local water wars, and failed crops as far as the eye could see. The contrast with his privileged life in Karnataka punctured his middle-class apathy and lit a fire that drove him to make a difference. He reached out to me when he recognised that one of my blogs was describing one of the *scenes* he had recently viewed. It was Rohit who came up with our name: the Witnesses. He wanted us to bear witness to what was happening, and help others to do the same.

So, then there were four of us. We were a great team. Cassie knew how to reach people and what would speak to different tribes. She looked at the tangled web of socials and could see where to pull a thread to keep building the momentum of a movement. She would analyse the streams and tell us what we needed to do next and she was usually spot on. My job was to come up with the words and images and she told me where to put them. She helped me build my followers exponentially but we also did a lot of work that wasn't public, joining conversations in the dark web, trying to open the eyes of those who were still just voyeurs of disaster. This was Rohit's domain, a network where he was respected. He got information where it needed to go, legally or otherwise. While we publicly told the stories of the climate-affected, he engaged in a more clandestine campaign, undermining the stories of the politicians and big business, and finding points of connection between disparate groups. And Aamira—she was the fire that drove us on. More than that, she recognised that we would never change the world through a socials campaign alone. For all of Cassie's skills, the socials' world was shallow and fickle. Someone might be struck by a *scene* and then shrug it off and be laughing at a cute puppy video a minute later. We needed other kinds of momentum.

"It's time" said Cassie's voice in my earbuds. "We need to hit now for maximum impact. Are you ready? And Rohit?"

"We're ready," I said. "What about Aamira?"

"I just heard from her, she's good to go."

"All right. Let's do this thing," I said. "Stay out of touch for at least 48 hours and then we'll take stock. See you on the other side."

I broke the connection and turned to my screen. My job was simple; I just had to hit publish on a blog piece. It felt like a big deal though. It was the first time I'd written about the *scene* that started it all for me, the Bangladeshi flood. More importantly, we were bringing the *scenes* into the mainstream. I had written openly about them and provided links to a painstakingly compiled and curated collection. Rohit had worked his wizardry—something to do with mirror servers I think—to make sure this public *scene* collection would be hard to take down. We were taking a big risk but Cassie assured us that the time was ripe and the public would be on our side. As soon as I published, Cassie was poised to get the piece out through all the socials, using all the tricks she knew to send it viral.

Aamira was already out on the streets, putting her piece of the plan into action. Rohit had pulled together a catalogue of climate crimes and linked it to our collection of *scenes*. It provided the facts on how much the biggest fossil fuel corporations had contributed to climate change and how long they had known about it without acting. Juxtaposed with the devastating reality of the *scenes*, it made compelling reading. I hit the publish button and I knew that Aamira was immediately signalling teams of well-trained activists to gather at the head offices of all of those corporations and make as much noise as possible - occupying, obstructing and protesting while the *scenes* were projected on walls and broadcast to sets for everyone to witness.

Of course, it wasn't just us. Four people can't change a world of eight billion. We were just one cell in something much bigger. We were all networked together through the dark web, to avoid surveillance and interference from the powers that be. We learned from each other, we disagreed, sometimes we undermined each other, but sometimes our discordant voices entangled in a symphonic moment that was bigger than any of us.

It was the work of decades, and it never really ends. Our movement grew too slowly and much was lost that should have been saved. There are no more tigers in the wild, most fisheries have collapsed, too many people have died. Yet, somehow, we're winning. The RegenTech sector is the powerhouse of our economies, delivering renewable energy and bio-mimicking technologies that recirculate materials and nutrients. Millions of people are working to re-forest the world and to bring food production into our cities. Most importantly, the vast majority of people, and the media, now agree that we need to transform our way of life to eliminate greenhouse gas emissions. The public and political debate has been won. There are still plenty of resisters but they've been driven to the fringes and lack real political power.

Groups like the Witnesses sprang up all over the planet and did whatever they could, whatever made sense to them, to wake up the world. The *scenes* played a pivotal role. We threw them into the mainstream but we used them to tell stories that would inspire empathy, not mere voyeurism. As socials took over from corporate media, everybody was sharing their worlds, building up webs of empathy as we all realised how our lives were entangled with each other and the planet. Something intangible shifted, at the level of our values and stories. The hollow promises of growth at all cost no longer rang true and we found ourselves increasingly seeking well-being in our connection with others, wherever they might be.

It was a turbulent and chaotic time. There was conflict and resistance, wins and losses. People clung to power and the many corporations that fell did great damage as they thrashed about in their death throes. But we continued to bear witness until a great global movement arose that swept away the old order. It was a movement that affirmed the value of life wherever it exists on our planet and eschewed practices that destroyed life. Eventually, marked by no particular day, it just became normal to think that way.

So now, we regrow the forests so that tigers may one day stalk the wilds again. For now, we only fish valuable plastic from the oceans, leaving fisheries to recover. We limit incomes in the rich world and use our resources to help those parts of the world where help is most needed. The planet and its people will take a long time to recover but there is a real sense of meaning, of purpose, in this great task of stewardship—regenerating the Earth.

People still make and share *scenes*, but they're different now. I'll share one of my favourites. A friend stitched it together from what he saw every day, for decades, as he walked out his front door. It tells a story of gradual change that adds up to something transformative.

I look out across a slum—filthy, chaotic, polluted, depressing. Very slowly, it starts to change. Ramshackle shanties are torn down and replaced with gleaming new buildings. Solar tiles appear on rooftops. Most noticeably, the colour changes—from greys and browns to myriad greens and blues, as nature is welcomed back into the city. A concrete stormwater channel transforms into a meandering stream, lined with trees. The buildings seem to grow along with the trees, vegetation creeping over them as it becomes part of the building fabric. Electric vehicles and bicycles appear, first many, and then fewer as an underground transit system clears the streets for walking and living. Birds and animals appear.

There is no moment of perfection in the *scene*. The transformed city is imperfect. One building is abandoned, the greenery in one lot has been neglected and dies, a solar panel is cracked. There is always still work to be done. Nevertheless, there is a moment during the *scene* when the realisation hits you that this is no longer the place it was. It creeps up on you. Suddenly, something about the colours is different, more vibrant—something new has emerged. I love that moment. I love that I witnessed it.

AUTHOR STATEMENT, CHRIS RIEDY

This story was inspired by the quantum idea of entanglement – a sense that if we could become more aware of the ways that our lives are entangled with other lives and places, our collective values would start to shift. There is particle-wave duality here too; the characters and world are both dark and light, depending on the angle.

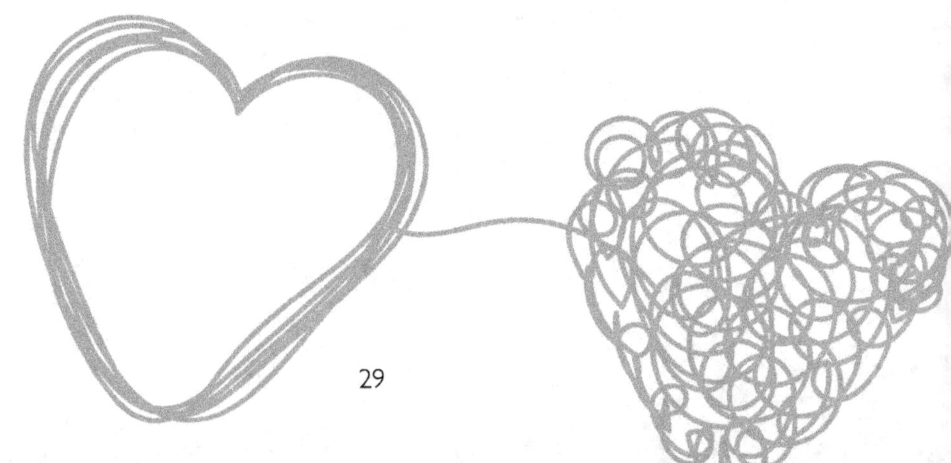

49%, or Polypropylene from the series, Rising Horizon
by © David Cass, davidcass.art

THE DROUGHT

by Jessica Wilson

Some say the place where the change began was Cape Town, a violent sprawling city at the tip of the African continent known for its beauty. Others disagree. There was no beginning. There was no single place, they say. Time wraps in on itself. Everything is connected.

It is true that there was a period when the rain didn't fall. For seven years in a row, the winter rains that usually fill up the kloofs and valleys of the Cape Fold Mountains didn't come. The fynbos barely noticed. Used to endless cycles of drought and fire, the plants making up the richest floral kingdom in the world continued to breathe and blossom. And, initially paying no heed to the cloudless skies, the residents of Cape Town topped up their chlorine-enriched pools and watered their English-green lawns. The dams surrounding the city shrank lower and lower as water poured out without flowing in. Eventually all the officials and machines and networks and politicians and monitoring equipment and forms that made up the city's neural network noticed. *We are going to run out of water!* They cried. The residents of Cape Town, until that point severed from the city's brain, as minds became severed from bodies in the post-industrial age, sat up and took notice. Their noticing echoed throughout the planet.

As if waking from a deep sleep, humans, who for centuries had channelled rivers, dammed valleys, chopped down forests, thrown poisons onto the earth, exhumed and burnt fossilised plants, rubbed their collective eyes and looked around them. It was not a pretty sight. The earth was parched. And where it wasn't parched, floods were amassing, fires raging, winds howling and the sea lapping hungrily at the land. *Poor us!* They cried. *What have we done to deserve this?* But the answer was there for all to see. They had disconnected their thoughts from their feelings, themselves from each other, their species from the web-of-life and their souls from the sacred. And they had projected this peculiar and sad form of reality onto a self-aware, living cosmos, of which they were a part.

Back in drought-stricken Cape Town, the place where the change may or may not have begun, the mayor proclaimed that Day Zero was imminent. She would order all home and business taps to be closed. The last drops of water in the dams would be rationed at collection points under military control.

And that, some say, is when it happened. The neighbourhood WhatsApp groups started to buzz:

- hi i'm samir dm me if you need help on day zero i'm strong & can borrow a bakkie no charge

- we collecting more rainwater than we need bring your buckets

- have a spring neighbours welcome to collect drinking water free

- compost loo DIY class sun 10am bring 2 buckets and a pool noodle no charge

These messages of love and solidarity soon crowded out the texts of fear and racism that had long dominated the groups. Emboldened by this new connection, neighbours soon smiled and waved at each other. They exchanged names. More miraculous still, the groups started to talk to one another. The razor wire walls and gated villages that separated people of different colour, language and religion were invisible in these cyber groups.

Before long the entire social fabric of the city changed. A young street-girl, hardened through weather and *tik,* picked a yellow daisy from a scrubby road-side bush. After staring at each unique petal she handed it with great care to a corporate executive who, for the first time ever, had lowered the tinted window of his gas-guzzling four by four at a traffic light. The man burst into tears.

A suburban trophy wife, obsessed with keeping herself young and uncontaminated by the wretched of the earth, dropped all pretence. She sought out unemployed youth, filled with the hopeless cynicism of their poverty-stricken birth. Together, against all odds they started a cross-city, cross-gender boxing gym where, through sweat and courage, members were forced to confront their prejudices and get to know each other.

Such things became common practice and, in the deep recognition of collective vulnerability, all power relations fell away. No one felt the need or desire to exploit anyone else. Generosity blossomed.

With common intent and purpose, as well as some breakthroughs in artificial intelligence, the need for cell phones disappeared. People could communicate with each other at will by switching on or off certain parts of their brains. Without the endless demand for rare earth elements, silver, gold and other minerals, conflicts around the world came to a halt. Children in central Africa were allowed to grow up without being initiated into child armies. Women were safe from the violence of men.

Or so the story goes.

Whether it happened in a moment or over centuries, no one could say. But everyone agreed that when the seas rose to their maximum height and the earth reached its hottest temperatures, things were different. The human species changed. The Age of Greed and Narcissim ended. And the time for cleaning up their mess began.

Karipi asked her grandmother to tell her the story again; the story her grandmother's grandmother had told her. The story that had been passed down by elders from a world no one could remember. It was hard to believe humans once had thought nothing of killing each other for an imaginary slight, or destroying an entire forest teeming with life for a thing called money. They had very nearly laid waste to the entire planet. Although incredulous, Karipi was also curious. She had dreams in which a vast and uncomfortable feeling swelled up inside her. The emotion was primal from a place that had no words. It rose unbidden, shape-shifting and terrifying. It felt the only way to escape it was to do a terrible thing, to really hurt someone. She told no one of these dreams.

"But what did it *feel* like to acquire a new transport-machine when you knew that it would kill all the coral?" She would ask of her grandmother, Sylvia. Or, "Were some people really allowed to kill other people just because they *looked* a certain way or thought certain thoughts?"

In Karipi's world everyone was a honey-brown colour and the belief in a single, judgemental God had long since vanished. Differences between people were celebrated in the same way that diversity of species was celebrated – both were critical to innovation, evolution and the long-term well-being of planet earth.

Sylvia could not answer Karipi's questions. They were not questions most children asked. She took them to the council of wise beings.

"She is being called," was their unanimous response, "her time is approaching." No deliberation was necessary.

Sylvia hid the news from her grandchild. She too started to experience unfamiliar emotions: attachment and denial; fierce love and protection; wishing Karipi's fate on another being. Most children experienced a minor transition into adulthood. For some, initiation was just a ritual, a celebration and welcoming. This would not be so for Karipi.

Sylvia's nights became restless and she started to walk. This simple activity had all but disappeared during the Age of Greed and Narcissism, especially amongst the wealthy classes. Now it formed the backbone of the Conscious Integral Age. By the simple mechanics of walking, neurons moved between the left and right sides of the brain, integrating pain and trauma before it could build new neural pathways that passed from generation to generation, resulting in dictators, genocides and climate change. The fact that Karipi's questions could not be answered through walking was a mystery to her grandmother. But every so often a child was born who expressed a gene sequence that was usually dormant, a message from the past: a memory.

Karipi stepped into the water. It was full moon and the tide had emptied out the sea. No waves crashed on the rocks. She was drawn down to the tidal pool in the middle of the night when she couldn't sleep. These pools were replicas of ones that had been around for centuries.

Mostly she sat on the tidal wall or nearby rocks trying to discern movement or sound, a hermit crab seeking a new shell, the wind rippling across the water. Once, just before dawn, she heard an otter digging in the sand. It was a miracle that this shy niche-creature had survived the onslaught of homo sapiens. A small smile had opened in Karipi's otherwise dark mind. Tonight though, things were uncannily still and quiet.

Turbulent emotions were common in the beginning of the Conscious Integral Age. As the organism developed that had once been billions of separate humans, intense destructive emotions were more rare. People worked with their dreams and feelings, and each person – for people were still individuals at the same time that they were part of a larger whole – was guided toward their role, the occupation that would transform the difficult parts of their personality into creative expression. Slowly but surely the collective greed, hatred and anger of human beings was purified, their karma cleansed. Or put another way, these destructive parts of human experience were integrated so that they didn't pass, unconsciously, from one generation to the next. Most children experienced a fraction of the rage, hatred and insecurity that their parents, grandparents and great grandparents had felt.

For Karipi though, the dreams had grown worse. Instead of just *feeling* hateful, she did terrible things. One night she took a knife to an antelope and slit its throat. In another dream, she beat someone with her bare hands until his body went limp. An inferno she unleashed swept through an entire settlement until not a single cockroach breathed. At these times her dreaming was not lucid and so she really believed herself capable of these wanton, horrible acts. And in her sleep-state she felt not remorseful but gleeful, powerful, invincible. Only when she woke did she feel conflicted. Her body contorted in knots. She looked at all the loving generous beings who surrounded her, at her wise, caring grandmother and felt ashamed. But behind or inside the shame was a strong curiosity, a shoot of imagination that could not be silenced a hunger for power: *what if I…?*

She sat on a rock in the centre of the pool, with her lower half submerged just below the surface of the water. The night air surrounded her from waist up. There was almost no difference in temperature between the two mediums but a very slight breeze across her torso gave her a rippling sensation. She paddled her feet slowly, creating a similar movement of feeling across her calves and ankles.

The night darkened as clouds started to gather around the moon. The sea swelled. Waves lapped at the far wall. Every fourth or fifth wave spilled into the pool, tiny droplets splashing the still water. She floated toward the sound, trying to lay her body exactly where the splash would land. So many times she got it wrong and started laughing. Soon though, every wave was crashing into the pool and it was impossible to avoid the piles of foam. It tickled her skin and her laughter turned to a deep contented smile, her body tossed gently this way and that. She lay face up, at one with herself and with the water.

Then, seemingly out of nowhere, a wave crashed onto her so hard that it took her breath away. Her ribs felt bruised as she gasped for air. The water was coming in too swiftly and strongly for her to swim to the far wall so she kicked sideways, searching with her hands for the side-wall's surface to grip on. For a moment her arms were pulled faster than her body, stretching her in the water. Her hips crashed into the rough wall, which was covered in urchins and barnacles. She shifted her weight to her lower body and slowly pulled herself back into the pool. A moment's hesitation and she would have been swept into the open ocean. The sky was now pitch black and it had started to rain. With the tide so high, there was no way out of the pool. She started to shake, her heart hammering, as her fingers sought to pull out the prickles embedded in her flesh.

Sylvia walked high into the mountains. She could hear her granddaughter's soul screaming and there was nothing she could do. She walked on.

It was not that the wise beings were all-powerful but that they were all-knowing. They were not pronouncing a punishment, but revealing an unfolding. Sylvia wished it were not so. Karipi's screams were inside her now. She walked with more deliberation. Left. Right. With each step she shifted her weight and visualised the neurons firing rapidly. Left. Right. Emotions poured into her body. Anger. Left. Right. Hatred. Left. Right. Jealousy. Shame. Annihilation. On, she walked.

Karipi's fingers were numb. Even so she could sense the bumps on her skin where her body fought the poisoned urchin tips. They would not come out now. She moved back to the centre of the pool, away from the current pushing across the walls into the vast unknown ocean. The rock where she had placidly sat was now deeply submerged. She could reach it with the tips of her toes and still keep her head above water. This tenuous grip held her in place while she battled to remember her lessons.

Since infanthood, all children were taught to work with their mind-body and emotions. A trickster at heart, Karipi had not always done her homework diligently. She had seen no need, preferring to run wild in the kloofs and cliff-faces. And the organism had let her run. Wildness, freedom, sensuality were all important elements of the whole. They came directly and unbidden through certain beings, refreshing the life of the collective. But now, in the pool, Karipi felt desperately alone, abandoned. She could not sense anyone, anything, any awareness. Her grandmother's steps were invisible to her. Silent. She fell into a fathomless space of pure terror where images flooded her mind. Huge buildings belched toxic smoke surrounded by a wasteland of dead earth; mono-species plantations stretched for miles and miles in which not a single bird sang; children, covered in blood and mud with guns longer than their torsos crept in terror through the shadows of dunes. These and more tumbled through her mind. And in each she was not only the observer, but also the last fish-eagle to be born, the child whose limbs were blasted off by a land-mine, the river desperately trying to rid itself of poisons, the oil baron who hanged himself. The feelings were unbearable. And still they came. Faster and faster, more and more intense until she had no idea who she was, or where. Her toes continued their tenuous grip on the rock as her body was pounded in every direction. A massive wave, bigger than all the others, came over the wall. Its reach was so long that it crashed directly on her with the full power of the deep ocean.

Sylvia stumbled. It took all of her being to keep going. Left. Right. She felt the weight of her granddaughter's limp body resting in her arms. With great care, she adjusted her posture so that her hands were high above her head. Even with the added strain in her shoulders, her breathing eased, just a little.

Karipi's mind was empty. There was nothing but space in every direction, below her, above her, to the north, south and east, and in directions she had never known existed. Gradually she became aware of a faint light. She tried to focus her eyes. Her body felt weightless and still; the terrible tossing had stopped. Something was holding her, its touch gentle. The light grew brighter as the moon emerged from behind clouds. Then suddenly the sky was clear and filled with billions of stars. She felt a slight movement beneath her and the faintest dropping of her heaviness. Very slowly she turned to look at what had been supporting her. The sea was translucent in the moonlight but she could see no shapes other than the rocks with which she was familiar.

Taking a deep breath Karipi dived down. There was space between the rocks and she kept going. And there, in front of her, drawing her, was an enormous moon-coloured ray. The water was soft and her swimming effortless. Without ever coming to consciousness, a memory rippled up from her pre-mammalian brain that allowed her body to adjust and take oxygen from the water. It felt the most natural thing in the world. On they swam, ancient ray and young girl, human-fish and fish-human.

After some time Karipi saw patches of bone-like structures beneath them. She paused to look more closely at the fine tendrils of white lattice. Bleached coral. Dead. It stretched ahead of her as far as she could see, the skeleton of a once living system, another victim of the ecocide unleashed by climate change. Her heart contracted and she started to weep. Copious salty tears, indistinguishable from the seawater, streamed down her cheeks, growing the ocean just a little.

In the vast expanse she saw one lone fish, small and brightly coloured. In its mouth was a piece of coral, not quite white. The fish had chosen a place where the dead lattice-work was tight, and using its body and mouth, manoeuvred this small living piece of sea life so that it was wedged and balanced. The task looked impossible. Yet as her eyes adjusted, Karipi saw that not everything was dead. In a few places, small branches of the lattice exuded faint colours. In that moment, she knew what she had to do.

At last Sylvia stopped walking. Her limbs were weary but her mind was clear. She felt the pain and turmoil that was Karipi's, that was hers, that was humanity's since beginningless time had eased. For a moment.

At home, she lay down on her bed and closed her eyes. Deep in the ocean, a giant moon-coloured ray lifted and lowered its wing-like fins for the last time and dropped down, down, down.

"Granny, granny," Karipi shouted as she came running into the house, her hair still wet. "I know what I must do! I've found my task, my calling, my *seriti*." She shed her wet clothing and bundled herself into a warm wrap. "It's the coral. I'm going to nurture the coral back to life. A fish showed me how and others will help me!"

Sylvia's door was open. Karipi's body-mind went perfectly still as she stood looking at the radiant smile on her grandmother's face. Sadness welled up inside her and tears flowed freely. But she felt no regret, no anger. Her grief was pure love and it radiated from her heart to touch every living being throughout the universe.

AUTHOR STATEMENT, JESSICA WILSON

A prolonged drought in Africa triggers quantum social change when residents cooperate rather than compete for scarce water. This shift in collective consciousness marks the end of the era that produced climate change and other horrors. Centuries later a young girl's rite of passage transforms vestiges of intergenerational unconscious trauma.

The Ephemeral Marvels Perfume Store
by © Catherine Sarah Young, theperceptionalist.com

THE EPHEMERAL MARVELS PERFUME STORE

by Catherine Sarah Young

A little brown mouse hopped out of the boat that had just anchored itself to the dock. Quietly, it skittered between the other boats whose owners had already retired for the night. Some new ones were brightly painted, while others showed decades of wear. The city was quiet and the moon glowed brightly.

The seas had risen long ago and had kept rising, until finally they leveled off. The world's giant leaking faucet had been sealed. Many families who had been living on large rafts formed a new marine colony. Years passed and floating cities dominated the waters, houses connected by sea bridges that served as a foundation for the city. The bridges held them all together in a network with "roads" that allowed them to easily go from one building to the next.

This city of Arana was anchored to the new seabed--the land where their great grandfathers used to plant crops. Now it served to hold the city together and keep it from floating away.

The mouse ran along a bridge that angled sharply to the left and onto another group of floating houses. This was the merchant district. The little mouse passed buildings where people sold fish, sea vegetables, and air-grown plants and flowers, before running straight into a dull-looking wooden structure at the edge of the city. Near the windows were bottles made of colored glass and filled with translucent liquid, which gave an interesting contrast to the building's gray color. The mouse paused behind a shelf and fell asleep.

Our little mouse had entered the residence and workshop of the city's perfumer.

The shop was plain compared to the others, which were decorated with large colorful geometric shapes. The walls were made of exposed wood and brick. Small, beautifully shaped glass bottles decorated the wall display. Above the door hung a large sign: *The Ephemeral Marvels Perfume Store.*

Emilia, the city's perfumer, was a simple and direct woman who poured all of her energies into the perfumes she was making. She was precise, quick-minded, and sensitive to the smallest changes in weather. She was also an insomniac, and tonight she was the only one in the city who was still awake. She sat at a long mahogany table at the far end with large distillation flasks, a metal weighing scale, measuring tools, and other equipment set out neatly before her. One could smell roses that shifted to hints of saffron, jasmine, and eucalyptus when moving from one end of the table to the other. A nearby shelf held large amber jars full of different essential oils. The shop was dark except for the desk lamp casting a bright yellow glow on the glassware. Emilia was carefully mixing a simple perfume for an important client. That's it, one more drop, she thought.

As the mouse came in, the floor creaked and Emilia sat upright. She removed her glasses and rubbed her eyes. She had been working on this perfume for ten days now and finally it was done. It was time to stop and get some much-needed rest. She carefully decanted the perfume into an emerald bottle and placed it in a box that the client would pick up tomorrow. Her fingers traced the amber jars, sealing them before standing up to place them back onto the shelf. Silently, she went upstairs to her bedroom and was soon sound asleep.

At the other end of the perfumery, the cat cautiously licked the spider webs growing on the alchemy jars, tasting the missing spider's last meals and the particles brought in by the winds from storms past. Sensing the cat, the sleeping mouse jerked awake and ran for its life, away from the perfumer's shop.

As the sun rose the next day, the city slowly shuddered to life. The fishermen were always up first. Each carefully detached the rope that held their boats to the dock and started the small engine that would take them to the more remote areas of the ocean that still had fish. About an hour later, the other merchants began to open their shops. Fruits and vegetables were expensive and grew only on roofs and vertical gardens. People shopped for seaweed, kelp, and other sea vegetables, as well as oysters and clams. Emilia usually awoke late in the morning.

At 9 AM, someone rang the bell. "Hello?" Emilia unlocked the door and opened it with a big smile, widening her eyes to pretend she had not slept only three hours. She forced herself to speak in a cheerful voice.

"Good morning, Mr. Schmidt. Lovely to see you. Your perfume is ready, please come in."

Mr. Schmidt belonged to one of the wealthier classes in the city. Like other people of affluence, he lived in the city's center, which was connected to the surrounding areas by longer bridges. One needed identification or a permit to enter. The houses were higher, to prevent storm surges coming in. It was rumored that some held personal aquariums. Others held rare gardens, as one could tell by squinting through the midday sun and seeing which roofs were green and which had more birds squatting, hoping to catch a fish.

Our perfumer housed birds on her roof, too. She enjoyed feeding some lost seagulls, crows, or even the occasional eagle. Oftentimes, they came back with their own offerings, which exasperated her as these turned into tiny piles of clutter on her roof.

Emilia took last night's experiment off the shelf and placed two drops of it on a piece of paper. Politely, she held it out for Mr. Schmidt, who took it and sniffed. His wrinkled face brightened.

"Yes, it's wonderful. Rose, vetiver, and … let's see … eucalyptus. My wife will love it."

Emilia beamed. "I'm glad you like it. Eucalyptus is one of my favorite essences. It's a pity it's difficult to get."

He smiled. "It will remind her of the delightful times we had when we were younger. Eucalyptus trees were plentiful then, weren't they?"

"They were, indeed." Emilia's parents, frequent travelers to other cities, had always taken their daughter along. She had a surplus of memories of things that most people had never experienced. This, plus a strong sense of smell, led her to take over her father's failing spice business and to become a perfumer when she was barely out of school. She started to preserve disappearing scents of trees and flowers in her childhood. Hence, *The Ephemeral Marvels Perfume Store*.

It was a lonely business at first, but as the storms and the drought persisted all over the world, Emilia's clientele grew. It started as a business for the wealthier people in the city because only they could afford such luxuries. As the years passed the climate continued to worsen, and the city lost more crops. Some species survived, such as herbs and spices that needed little care to grow, and some hardy vines. But more species did not make it. She had a special set of essential oils of scents that were once common but were now very rare.

Eventually, she brought the prices down a bit during some seasons because everyone wanted perfumes of things they could no longer smell in the natural world. Before living on a floating city, the land used to be rich with trees, and people missed the scent of cedar. Older people wanted to recall the memories of their youth when there was much more to smell, such as the scents of older varieties of fruits and flowers, and the odors of seasons when they were more distinct. Younger ones wanted new experiences, though Emilia was saddened that they would never get to smell a field of lavender or a beach with coconut trees. Sometimes when business was very good, she would hold open days when children could come to the workshop and make their own perfumes for free.

"Also, my wife wanted to give you these." Mr. Schmidt handed her a large package wrapped in paper. Emilia unwrapped it and saw with delight that they were fresh lilies.

"Lilies! I haven't seen one in months. How lovely, thank you!"

"We had a holiday way up in the north. The city didn't float; it used to be a desert and now they have rains every year. They grow lots of flowers we don't have here."

"Well, please make sure to send her my gratitude."

Emilia was always worried about running out of certain materials, but thankfully there were travelers from other cities that sold what she needed, or friends, like Mr. Schmidt, who gave her raw material. Although many times it wasn't nearly enough, and she would find herself waiting for months for the next traveler. Of course, this made procuring the essential oils inconsistent. Emilia was proud of her work and usually refused to sell such impure scents except during desperate times.

But thankfully she would have essence of lilies by this month's full moon.

Being a perfumer wasn't so different from being a monk. During the mornings, Emilia sold perfumes, then closed after lunch so that she could perform her experiments. The rest of the afternoon consisted of long periods of intense concentration, the careful weighing of material, and boiling water to steam so that the essential oil was pushed out. Distillation was painfully slow, one drop at a time for hours.

Or sometimes, like with lilies, she extracted their essence using *enfleurage*. She placed fresh petals on fat-soaked glass and sealed them into airtight wooden plates. Over the next several days, the fat would absorb the fragrance of the lilies. Emilia would then replace the petals and repeat the process until the fats had absorbed all of the bouquet's essences. Encased in fat, the essence of the lily would then be liberated using a solvent.

While waiting, Emilia would talk to herself, the cat, or the birds on her roof. When, finally, the remaining material looked devoid of anything useful, she would stop the process and place the small volume of liquid in a tiny amber bottle.

When the sun had set, after she had eaten her supper, she would mix essential oils to create perfumes. By then, the early evening breeze had cleared the air of the day's activities—a sign her nose took as being ready for her olfactory experiments.

Emilia had a thick notebook with the recipes of all the perfumes she had ever made in her life. While she sometimes made perfumes with only two or three notes, she was also famous for having some with a list of at least thirty ingredients. She had pipettes that were accurate up to 0.1 microliter. If she faced all of her perfumes, she could distinguish each of them and remember the occasion for which it was mixed. Her perfumes were like dear companions in these lonely times of uncertainty and loss.

One hot afternoon--Emilia hated hot days, because she worried for the essential oils--she heard a knock on the door.

Irritated, she spoke loudly through the door. "I'm sorry, we're closed. Please come back tomorrow morning."

The stranger knocked once again, louder this time. "I'm afraid I need your services immediately, Madame," a deep voice said.

Emilia remained firm. "We're closed, sir."

The man kept knocking and, sighing impatiently, Emilia opened the door a crack, ready to give the man a lecture on respecting the business hours of small enterprises. The stranger pushed his way inside. He was giant hulk of a man and Emilia was afraid he would knock over her bottles, or her. The mysterious man closed the door behind him. Emilia sputtered at his rudeness and placed her hand inside her pocket, readying the small knife she always carried with her.

"Excuse me, sir, but I'm afraid you have to leave!" She placed her free hand on her hip.

To her surprise, the man got down on his knees and folded his hands in supplication. Emilia studied him closely. He was large and seemed even bigger because of the animal fur he was wearing. One did not need such clothing in Arana; he was definitely not from around here. She sniffed the air and smelled his fear.

"My name is Frederico Salles. Forgive my trespassing, but I must see you immediately. It is a matter of life and death."

Emilia paused and took a deep breath. She relaxed her grip on her knife. Only a little bit.

"Alright. What do you want?"

Frederico wiped his brow and loosened his coat, as though just realizing how warm it was today. "I need you to create a perfume for me. A special one."

"You couldn't wait until tomorrow?"

"No, I'm afraid I could not. My sister is very ill, and we have come a long way. She is dying, and it is her wish to smell a particular scent before she leaves this world. Our city has no perfumers. It is very cold and nothing grows. It has been a very long journey, and your city was the first we encountered."

Frederico stumbled into her workshop, eyeing her bottles and her tools with wild eyes. Emilia grasped her knife tighter, alarmed. She started to draw her weapon, but something about him allowed her to let him keep talking.

"You can imagine how happy I was to learn that a perfumer lives here! My doctors believe that granting her wish might help her live longer, perhaps even cure her. I implore you, for the sake of my dying sister, please make her this perfume!"

Emilia's brow furrowed as she looked hard at her unusual customer. She decided he wasn't a threat and, while she didn't like being interrupted, she had also lost loved ones. She took a deep breath, released her knife, then walked to her desk and grabbed a piece of paper and a pen.

"Very well. I will make this perfume for you. Tell me what your sister desires."

The man told her, and the perfumer took notes. It was a long time before he finished talking. When he did, Emilia was silent.

Frederico's sister Carmen used to be one of the most celebrated dancers of her time. She had been athletic and graceful, jumping across the stage with a sensitivity and elegance that made a famous critic weep during one performance. Her career spanned decades, peaking at a show when she had played Giselle.

Frederico spoke wistfully. "The opening night for that season was my sister's happiest moment in her life. The entire family was there, including all of her children who were alive and well, and her dancing was legendary. Before she dies, she wants to remember that night."

Emilia was silent for several moments.

The woman wanted a perfume that smelled of her best performance.

Before he left, Frederico gave her a letter that detailed how Carmen remembered that evening. Emilia's fingers traced pages that outlined the dresses worn by the dancers down to the color and material, the music, the leather chairs of the audience, the wood of the stage. Her account was incredibly vivid, down to what she felt during each act and the flurry of activity backstage. Carmen's story transported her to another time.

Emilia paced the shop. And paced. And paced. She threw up her hands. She hadn't made a perfume like this in so long. And in these times, it was asking the impossible.

Emilia's eyes squinted as she carefully listed all the materials she needed. She thought deeply, checking her list with her inventory of essential oils and materials. After several minutes, she was breathing easier. She did have most of the oils that she needed, and as for the others, it was possible to create them. Except when she looked at the last item on the list.

Coffee. Carmen had described rich, black, dark roasted coffee after her performance, when she was backstage and before her husband met her with a large bouquet of lilies. (Thank goodness for the lilies Mrs. Schmidt sent, she thought.) But coffee. It was virtually extinct as far as she knew. In Arana, the last cup was drank thirty years ago, and now the people relied on other things to keep themselves awake. Rumor was that coffee was still grown deep in the south of the globe that used to be covered in ice. It had warmed, and the deathly cold was replaced by a chilly breeze. Now *Coffea arabica* thrived in the once frozen part of the world.

But those were just rumors. And Emilia could not travel. This perfume had to be made as soon as possible.

Emilia placed a sign on the front door that said, "Closed until further notice." Frederico had given her enough funds as a deposit, enough to keep her focused on this singular task. He essentially made me an employee, she fumed. What is it with rich people who think that money can stop time for them? A part of her regretted saying yes, but it was too late now. She was in such a rush that she didn't even bother to straighten the sign.

For the next several weeks, she labored. She brought out her arsenal of essential oils and set aside the ones she needed. Many of the scents on her list were rare or extinct; as far as she knew only she had the last of their essential oils. She scoured the markets for flowers, textiles, and other materials for the scents she still needed to produce. After six weeks, she was exhausted but she had 71 unique essential oils that she needed for Carmen's perfume. She had everything, except the one.

With only one missing ingredient, Emilia came out of her exile and searched the shops for coffee beans. She visited her wealthy clients and made requests, citing the importance of the matter, with no success. No one in her city had drank coffee in years. Children only knew it from textbooks that detailed those things the planet had lost.

Emilia did not want anything missing from her perfume. But how to make a perfume out of nothing?

Hearing the birds on her roof, she decided to go upstairs for fresh air. It would be good to have some company. As she climbed the stairs, she thought that perhaps she should make the trip down south and take her chances and maybe she would find a city where coffee was still available.

She reached the roof, lost in thought.

The birds had, as usual, brought their gifts. Emilia huffed in annoyance, and decided to clean the roof to clear her head. It would feel good to fix a tiny problem. Absentmindedly, she ran her hands over the hodge-podge of leaves, branches, stones, and other trinkets. One crow stood amidst the piles of avian offerings, pecking at something insistently. Curious, Emilia crawled closer.

Her eyebrows shot up, and her long fingers plucked at the pile. She inspected what looked like a brown bead, placed it near her nose and inhaled deeply. It was, unmistakably, a coffee bean. Excitedly, she went on all fours to examine the rest of the piles that had grown higher and higher for several weeks. It took hours of deep searching and dusk was falling rapidly. Worse, she smelled a storm coming. Her back ached, but evenutally she stretched her neck triumphantly. She found a total of twenty-seven coffee beans, perhaps the last ones in the world.

Emilia smiled ruefully at the birds' gifts, which she had long ignored but had contained treasures, and stumbled back downstairs.

Frederico came rushing into the shop, his bulk shaking the perfumery's foundations and waking up the last of the birds on her roof.

"You have it?" he asked, breathless.

Wordlessly, Emilia pointed to a velvet box on her desk. His big hands were surprisingly delicate as he opened it and lifted an amber bottle. He clutched it tightly with both hands and looked at it so intently, as though that one bottle carried with it all the hope in the world. His eyes shone, and Emilia's heart thumped. She swallowed the lump in her throat.

"Thank you. My sister will be very happy."

"Her condition is worse?"

Her client slowly shook himself out of his trance. "Much. When she's awake, she talks only about her dancing days. She talks to herself a lot. Sometimes, I think she's talking to her audience."

"I found all that was in your letter. I hope this works," she said.

Frederico left as fast as he had come in. Emilia sighed as she shut the door, her shoulders slumped and her eyes suddenly heavy. She didn't bother removing the "Closed" sign. She needed to take the rest of the day off.

A week later, Emilia was at the market when she heard one of the merchants sigh at the rarity of another of his wares: grapes. He only had a few baskets of them and wasn't sure when he would get any more.

Emilia frowned, then walked over to him and bought everything he had. She knew the next perfume she would be making.

AUTHOR STATEMENT, CATHERINE SARAH YOUNG

I use the abstract yet scientific relationship between scent and memory as a way for humans to redefine their relationship with nature through remembering their personal histories and reinforcing their identities, which can facilitate quantum social change.

Untitled by © Kristin Bjornerud and Erik Jerezano, kristinbjornerud.com

Synergy

by Otter Lieffe

Fog blanketed the heath and the early morning held its breath. There was no wind, not even the smallest of breezes, and the air hanging over the boggy earth was thick with anticipation.

Two teal ducks appeared out of the wall of white and landed loudly on a pond. They called to each other between mouthfuls of pondweed, a gentle sound that bubbled out of their chests, almost stolen by the heavy air. They could only just make out the shape of their friend on the water, but calling, they stayed connected.

The marshland had everything they needed, but today they were on edge, turning constantly on the cold water to keep watch. Their home was full of the stench of danger. A predator had passed by in the night, maybe a whole pack, and the scent of them lay in lines across the land. The water wasn't deep enough to keep the teals safe and they both knew it.

From the edge of the forest, a snatch of a cry reached their ears—a bear searching for her cub. Early dragonflies buzzed from pond to pond and the air resonated with the 'chack chack' of the first stonechat, taking his place on a branch of heather. No-one could know that in a thousand years this would all be concrete, parliaments, motorways and plastic bags.

The ducks had eaten their fill and, still calling to each other, they took off from the pond and flew out into the fog. The sky was lighter now and their day was just beginning.

Brussels: from the old Dutch for 'Home on the Marsh'.

The peregrine twisted, banked left towards sunrise, dropped down into the street. Another humid morning. If it stormed again, she would need to stay home—and the pigeons would be hiding too. Each day she carried the heavy bodies of birds to the nest, and each day her chick remained unsatisfied.

But she knew her hunting grounds like she knew the fluff on her young one's face. She made a loop around the tower of a decaying church and out into an avenue. A tramline ran a hundred metres below, a brook of rusty metal that led down and into the park. She went high again to take in her territory.

Even on a morning as burning hot as this one was sure to be, this was the perfect place to hunt. Acres of green grassland for the starlings to roam. The few poplars left unfelled were filled with the squawks of ring-necked parakeets. And squatting luxury towers of apartment buildings, there were enough pigeons to feed all the hungry peregrine chicks in the city.

When she was young, this had all been a construction site that seemed like it would never end. Squares of concrete connected by curving lines of cars, stinking trucks and screaming motorbikes. Even the pigeons had tasted like smog back then. But something had changed and now things were quiet. Roads replaced by gardens. Construction, by reclamation. She swerved over a line of fruit trees tended by a small group of humans. She couldn't be less interested in fruit or humans, but the trees attracted the food birds. And the food birds kept her chick quiet, at least for a while. She hovered for a moment and selected her prey—a male woodpigeon courting a female, flapping around, oblivious to her watchful presence in the sky. As the humans walked away with their baskets full, she pulled back her wings, narrowed her eyes and began her dive.

There's the falcon again. The third time that week she had watched her hunting over the gardens.

"Beautiful, isn't she?" Her friend appeared from behind a thick current bush, his basket overflowing with plump fruit. "You know, I think they're nesting earlier every year." Maria nodded vaguely. She loved the peregrines and she also knew they shouldn't be nesting this early. The tail end of the winter had been eaten by a precocious spring. Following closely would be another impossibly hot summer that would end, as summers did now, in fits and bursts somewhere in November. The falcons still hunted, the cherry trees still blossomed but the rhythms of the land were profoundly broken.

She turned to face the sun, peeking out between the tower blocks. Halfway up one of those grey buildings, she could easily see their home—the squatted apartments were ringed with the bright green of hanging gardens. *We've changed too,* she mused.

Wiping her brow on a sleeve, she mumbled to her bushes. *But will it ever be cold again?*

She picked a fat blackcurrant and popped it into her mouth—juicy and sweet and not nearly enough to quench her thirst. She lifted her head to look for the peregrine, but the sky was gone, consumed by greasy storm clouds closing in from the east.

Sighing, she lifted her heavy basket and as the first splatter of hot rain fell on her face, she stepped onto the path that led back to the tower, to her community, and the heat-insulated walls of home.

The waters were rising again. He could feel the change all around his scales, the tiny eddies and swirls and the subtlest increase in pressure on his gills. For a sensitive perch, it felt like his whole world was changing. He had to push harder with his tail to keep up with the current. He had already caught three other fish that morning—two roach and a minnow—but if the canal burst its banks again, he'd have to work a lot harder to catch another. The pounding of rain on the surface had been getting more powerful all day and his home was changing. He was strong, and he would adapt. His will to live, to survive, was everything.

He was moving now, and he knew the canal was escaping, bloated with rainwater, pouring over the concrete edge, through the broken wall and out into the king's park. For a while, the perch resisted the pull, his back braced, until the pressure began to send shivers down his spine and his fins burned with the effort. He let himself be taken and the current was incredible.

Within seconds he was flushed through a hole in the wall, barely avoiding a lethal line of barbed wire. A field of green passed below him; he was flying. He wanted to look down, to take in this bizarre new experience but nearly collided with a tree. He swerved around the massive trunk and swam out into the park.

He could taste other waters joining now. A goldfish pond absorbed into this expanding lake. An exploded water main that had irrigated the king's roses for a century. The perch could even taste the drowned bushes and herbs mixing in with the stagnant canal waters. Still pulled along by the current, he soared through the private gardens, swerving around statues and monuments—remnants of the long-forgotten dynasty of kings and some of the worst atrocities in African history.

This park belonged to the animals now, the perch and the roach and—

A flash of electric blue above him. A colour so intense he felt it pulse through his nervous system. Fear. Defense. Panic. He was already swimming down towards the grass below him, but the waters were too shallow. He wiggled down into a patch of nettles bent over in the current and he knew it wasn't enough. He looked for something better. Too late. A collision as a mouth closed in around him. A cold, hard beak that was already dragging him up and out of his element. Air, harsh and cold and all around him. His body going into shock, he felt it shutting down, pain-killing endorphins flooding his little body. This was how it ended.

She landed silently at her favourite willow branch, still the perfect spot for fishing despite the floods. She quickly finished her meal. Today was an easy hunting day, and she was full. She had never hunted on this side of the wall before because there had barely been water—or fish—here.

But with all that food trapped in a few shallow centimetres of water, nothing could be easier.

Normally, she hunted by the river and out of sheer curiosity, she took flight in that direction. Her belly almost hurt from the sheer amount of food inside it, but she flew fast and free in that direct way that kingfishers do, through the beech trees, over the bloated canal and to her regular spot. She landed on a branch slick with rain and took in the scene.

Here ran the last few metres of the Senne. Normally it was an insipid little flow, a distant echo of the great river choked into a canal and buried beneath sidewalks. Today the river was alive again, churning and crashing below her.

The little kingfisher knew it would be impossible to hunt in these conditions, but her belly was also too full to care. Transfixed by the sound of raging waters, she felt her eyes growing heavy. Despite the pounding rain and the incredible changes to her world, she tightened her grasp on the branch and slept.

It was time to move. She knew it, her children knew it. Their bags were packed and piled up by the door, just out of reach of the rising waters. She wore her tallest boots and her children were dressed and fed, each of them with as much food stuffed into their backpacks as they could carry. She knew her neighbours would be waiting for her to knock on their door and she knew they all needed to get moving before the river that used to be her street got any higher.

And yet she couldn't find the will to pick up the suitcase and start walking. They stood, the three of them, in their perfectly clean kitchen listening to the rain hitting the window. Her youngest was getting bored and had threatened to unpack her bag on the floor. Her eldest had his arms crossed and stared into space—a sure sign that he was already frustrated with her.

The discussions were over. Three nights had passed since her kids had sat with her on the new leather sofa in front of the evening news. Three nights since the sea crashed through her country's defences, since the dyke had breached live in front of a worldwide audience, since an entire city had been flooded and the cameraman had been swept away and barely survived. She knew her family was destined for a new life away from this town, and away from these low lands of her birth. And she knew time was running out.

She knew all of this and yet her feet were still glued to the pristine tiles of the kitchen floor.

Her youngest sighed dramatically, stepped forward and tried to pick up the biggest of the suitcases. It was almost as tall as she was, and she grunted as she tried to edge it towards the open door, legs splayed out like a frog, making her mother laugh despite herself. She stepped forward and easily lifted the case by its handle. The spell was broken, and their migration began.

Turning to switch off the light, she took one last look around their home; the opened doors of emptied cupboards, the new cheese plant from the supermarket that would surely die without them. Her children held each other's hands and with a resolute nod, she stepped out and led her family into the night.

Ten million people were on the move. Motorways were blocked with abandoned cars—obstacle courses for an entire country making their way to safety. As they marched south, the ten million combined with another movement of people, continuing a journey that had started months ago south of the Mediterranean and east of the river Jordan. Columns of people, kilometres long, streamed across a border that no longer existed. There was just water. The storms blowing in from the coast did nothing to slow them, the torrents of rain only gave them more determination.

They all had the same goal—to reach the inland capital that had promised safety and asylum, reversing a century of the policies of Fortress Europe.

At the end of the second day of their journey, the family stopped under a motorway overpass to eat and rest for the night. They were only half a day from the city, but she knew they couldn't walk anymore. Her feet hurt and her youngest was exhausted. She wasn't the first: there were already nearly a hundred people settling in and the concrete overpass echoed with voices.

She pulled an extra-large picnic blanket out of her backpack and laid it on a dry patch to mark her territory. Her youngest pulled off her wet shoes and started digging snacks out of her backpack while she looked around for her other child. That morning, like every morning, they had argued, and he'd stormed off to walk by himself. She had kept a close eye on him during the day and had seen him walking with another family. She saw him with them now, on the other side of the overpass, laughing.

With a broad, peace-making smile she beckoned him over. He nodded and started walking towards her. Then she realised her mistake. *He's bringing the other family with him.*

Instinctively she pulled her backpack full of food a little closer. It wasn't that she didn't want to share, she just had to look out for family first. If they started sharing their food, they would never have enough to get them to the capital. And besides, how could she trust them?

I'm not racist, she told herself. *But danger is danger and family comes first.*

As the foreigners approached, she wanted to politely make an excuse about the food—to explain that she'd *love* to share, it just wouldn't be possible— but as they came closer, a new language fell on her ears, her words froze on her tongue and before she knew it, her blanket was full of strangers.

Her kids emptied their backpacks and were already passing around their snacks to the newcomers. She started biting her nails and silently calculating kilograms and days and calories. She had to do something. She had to—

Just then, with a cheer that made her frayed nerves jump, the new family started emptying their backpacks onto the picnic blanket too. Bread and canned goods appeared. Some green lumpy fruit that she had never seen before. Two big bottles of water and plastic cups and a thermos—incredibly—of hot tea. Her youngest investigated a pile of chocolate bars with a grin and her mother relaxed a little. Still watching them carefully, she leaned back and let her children eat.

An hour later when they had had their fill, she lay out sleeping mats on the concrete and curled up with her children. An older woman appeared and offered her an extra blanket without a word. She accepted it with what she hoped was a grateful smile and lay it over her kids. As best she could, she tried to make her family comfortable and pulled her daughter close enough to feel her pulse and hear her breath. Curled up under a motorway, surrounded by hundreds of strangers, the mother never closed her eyes.

It was too much. The crowds of noisy, shouting humans hurt him. His entire nervous system was buzzing with too many soundwaves crashing onto his body. Too much. Too much. He had to get away.

His was a quiet life, a dark world of echoes and the occasional squeak of a friend or the rustle of a tree branch or the flap of panicking food. These new voices were unbearable, and he needed to leave.

As he escaped his home, followed by a few hundred of his community, the bat noticed two things—the rain had stopped, and the world outside of the underpass was also full of people. He flew low to take in the scene and as his echoes came back to him, he could already tell that the motorway, abandoned for months, was full of people walking, people using wheelchairs, people carrying bags. He was curious, but the noise had left him disorientated and overwhelmed. He headed south.

He needed to be somewhere familiar. Flying to his favourite pond, he could almost taste the crunch and dust of moths in his mouth. The hunting was always good there and he salivated with anticipation. But as he arrived and pushed out his echoes, he knew everything here was wrong. The pond was gone, or better said, the landscape was gone and had *become* the pond. The base of his favourite oak was inundated and the moths, usually concentrated over the still waters, were spread out, impossible to catch.

The bat made a loop around the trees and... nothing. He picked up the squeaks of another bat but she too sounded empty, hungry. This was becoming a bad night for all of them.

Then he felt something. He sensed a moth—and a big one at that—buzzing around the branches of a poplar. He swung in for the kill. The echoes vibrated the tiny hairs of his prey who ducked between leaves to hide. The bat swerved to catch him, but the moth slipped between two branches. The bat barely avoided a collision and at the last second, he pulled up and away.

The hunt was over in microseconds and the bat's stomach gave a frustrated rumble. Making one final loop he gave up on the pond and headed out towards the city.

They were back. Every night the moths arrived in droves drawn by the hanging gardens and night-blooming nicotinas. And every night they were distracted from their meal by the allure of candlelight—their fuzzy bodies crashing against glass, unable to resist. Attracted by their frustrated sounds, the hunters soon followed.

Tiny silhouettes of pipestrelles diving in and disappearing into the darkness, too fast for Maria's eyes to follow them. Her face pushed up close to the window, she looked down, past the balcony to the street, seven floors below. More arrived every day since their gardens had become a lake, since the Senne had been reborn, since Brussels had become a world of water.

Another sound reached her ears. More banging, she noticed, but far too loud to be moths. She turned on her heels and saw the panicked expressions of her friends. Someone was outside their apartment knocking hard on the door and the sound was getting louder.

But we're the only squatters here.

And we look ridiculous. Academics brandishing baseball bats. Hippy parents pointing toy guns. Writers and organic gardeners and philosophy professors with bottles and kitchen knives and anything else they thought might look like a weapon. They were a middle-class army that could terrify nobody. But it would have to do.

Maria stood closest to the door. They had no leaders, but they all knew that she'd be the one. Five years before, when the city had fallen into chaos, they had squatted this building as a collective, but she had been the first to turn the key. An unfinished tower of unfinished flats, luxury apartments for an elite that had never arrived. Retreating as high up as they dared, they had taken four floors for themselves and built a new life tending their hanging gardens and watching as down below everything had changed. Their community safely forgotten in the sky, they had never had to defend their home. Until today.

She pushed her shoulders back. "Who's there?" she shouted, her voice breaking a little. "This is *our* home!"

The knocking stopped but no-one replied. She heard only the continued pounding of insects throwing themselves against glass.

"I said…who's there?"

"We need help," came the reply. "The water…rises. Please…"

Maria looked at her friends and colleagues, her new-found family. They looked back at her, just as uncertain. Her hands were shaking so much she nearly dropped the keys, but she knew they would all expect her to decide.

She swallowed, bit her lip and opened the door.

The squat was full, just as the motorway underpass had been the night before. And just like the underpass, so many wet clothes and shoes and bags and umbrellas and jackets and sleeping bags and soaked, exhausted human bodies, turned the air into soup. Every stove in the building was being used to heat water, the back of every chair was being used to dry out someone's life.

There was space, but only just. There would be food, but only just. Translation was already becoming an issue and without communication, Maria knew things would get complicated, fast. They would have to share everything they had and create whole new solutions to whole new problems. They would have to find a way forward, together.

The first meeting had already been called for the morning. As she walked around the apartment, Maria saw a family had taken on kitchen responsibilities—a mother who looked tired to her bones was organising pots and pans and her kids were helping the best they could. Within an hour she'd built a team of ten people to prepare breakfast and, satisfied that the world would continue turning without her, the mother found a wooden chair in a corner and collapsed.

Maria stepped into the corridor. She saw a chart on the wall and next to it, a pen dangled from a piece of string tied to a picture hook. There must have been a painting here, but for the life of her, she couldn't remember which one. She leaned closer to read the chart and realised the only words were people's names—written in various alphabets—and the rest was all hand-drawn sponges and buckets, toilets and showers. She took the pen and signed herself up for cleaning for the next two days.

As she turned and went back into the living room, she noticed that an increasing number of people moving around the apartment were wearing envelope labels on their arms. Someone must have found them in the office and had been distributing them. Puzzled, Maria waited for someone to hand her a box of labels and with gestures and words, they made her understand. Write down the languages you speak, put the label here so everyone can see: a translation system had been born.

She headed to the balcony, her head pounding with logistics, her body buzzing with so many new emotions.

The careful organisation of their collective was being taken apart piece by piece and rebuilt to include new ways of being. Maria knew that the quiet life they had built in the tower would never be the same, but she also knew they had made the right choice. And, after all, change was the only constant any of them had ever known.

The sun was rising through the busy skyline and the last of the moths had gone to wherever moths go. Maria threw open a door and stepped out onto the balcony. They were between showers and, full of the thickest clouds and the brightest reds, the sky was so dramatic it almost hurt.

She rubbed her sleepless eyes and a shadow passed over her balcony. She heard the sounds of cooing and flapping—the thousands of pigeons living above them were just preparing for their day. Which meant the falcon was just beginning her hunt.

For some reason she couldn't explain, the thought gave Maria hope. That no matter how much things changed, no matter how much their lives were disrupted, some cycles continued. She turned her back on the city and, smiling for no good reason, stepped back inside to start again.

Author Statement, Otter Lieffe

Although we forget it at our peril, humans are one integrated part of a vast ecological system. We are connected—entangled and involved— and objectivity is pure myth. Social change, like all change, is messy and uncertain; full of potential. This story embodies some of that glorious complexity.

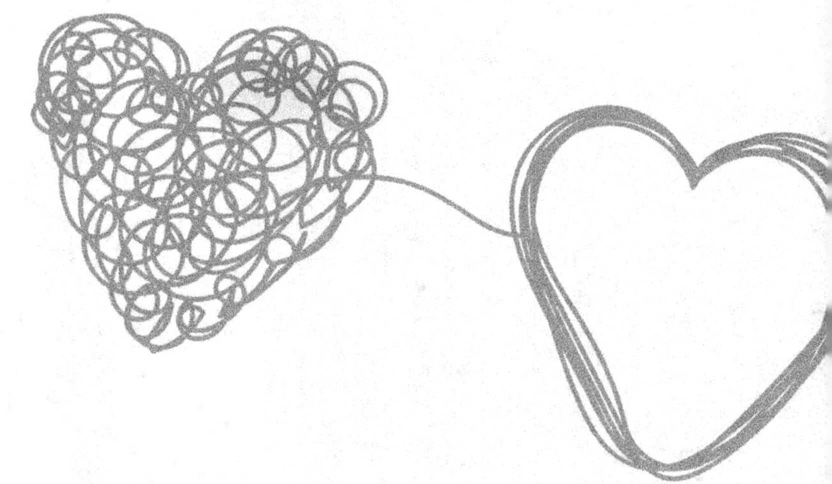

Three Pines by © Danielle Eubank, danielleeubank.com

Cool Burn and
the Cherry Ballart

by Jude Anderson

Ado said this.

From the shade of a White Cedar, on the banks of the Shoalhaven River which rose in Australia's Great Dividing Range and plunged 327 kilometres through Yuin Nation ancestral lands to emerge into the Pacific Ocean at Nowra, Ado said:

"There's no difference. My people, our story, Wandi Wandian clan, how we connect to country, respect it, our law, our language, creation stories, it's all one. We learn here on Country. Dharrawal language Country. On special sites."

It was never 'Terra Nullius' – a legal status declaring land unoccupied which conveniently paved the way for its colonization.

Five generations back, settlers arriving by boat like my ancestors had not often shared – they'd taken. And here, they'd massacred and taken. Two hundred years ago, here near the tree, settlers with their sense of entitlement had massacred Ado's elders to strip his clan's country of their tendered timber cedars, and construct and furnish the now classified heritage buildings of a rising class of landed gentry and governors with a rare and beautiful wood; wood from the White and Red Cedars sacred to Ado's sixty thousand-year-old living culture. Being twisted, the huge tree we were sitting under had survived.

Ado said: "Before I do anything in Country – use the water, get some food, collect plants, I speak to it, you know, to show respect."

"Does what you say change with what you're doing?"

"I just say thanks."

"How do you say thanks in Dharrawal?"

"Just quietly, under my breath."

We laughed…

"Yudunji".

It was Thursday December 6th, 2018. I was part of a small group of artists and academics working with an esteemed climate change scientist we had met eighteen months earlier at a Water Futures symposium. We'd needed more time together and I had proposed a residency at Bundanon Farm. It felt important to be close to water - to be in Country rather than on it; a way of bringing Country 'into' us to find expression for our 'Water Future'. Rather than beginning our residency where we'd left off, I'd proposed we begin by shifting our practice to feel 'deep time and Country' by embracing a First Nation people's perspective on place. It was a gut feeling I had, and it felt vital. The shift could potentially bring an enriched focus and questioning to our project. It was a field unknown to us and I had no idea how this would play out, but I hoped the knowledge and connection it offered could bring new meaning and vitality to how we worked. It was a way of igniting a fire and perhaps trusting we'd find our way through the smoke.

We were now sitting with Ado in the quietude of a riverbank which framed the farm's southern boundary. Violent storms had ripped through the area one week beforehand. The build-up season in the far north had spilled into the first cyclone whose southern reach was long. But now it was hot, still, and apart from the pulse of cicadas and the metronome beat of the bronze winged pigeon's sigh, it was quiet. Ado looked across the river to the opposite bank.

I dug my right foot into the cool of the sand and watched a mosquito draw blood from my arm. In the calm of Ado's gaze, I thought of the settler violence. The noise. The noise of violence; the bloodletting, timber felling, the loss. And then Ado whispering to Country in Dharrawal. On the cleared farm fields to the river there was a stone homestead, cattle, kangaroos, a recent plantation of native plants and trees, a vast mat of couch grass and a plague of wombats. After the rains in the seasonal heat and among the animals, Ross River virus could be circulating again. I flicked the mosquito away.

"Sometimes I touch it – whatever I'm collecting or using or sharing. Sometimes I touch it and say 'Thanks.'"

"…And then you drink it or eat it – share it."

"…Yeah."

"How do you know how much you can take?"

"We just take what we need. Others come after, you know, so we drink and eat, collect medicine, keep warm - just take what we need. And then, depending on the season, whether it's a good one…you read it – what you can take, what you leave. You read what's been left so you can let it regenerate. If you found a big pile of oyster shells – you'd catch fish."

More than fish I loved oysters. Some of the best oysters I'd ever eaten were from Ado's country. This love had led me well out of my comfort zone to Greenwell Point near Nowra where tin sheds slouched on a shell grit peninsula among the mangroves, and local suppliers with names like 'Jim Wild' rumbled around on forklifts batching their oyster hauls for city restaurants. Heat, sweat, rust, mud flats, sharks, snakes, stingrays, mosquitos and oysters. In the thick of river delta-country the 'make do' was pushed hard. I trod lightly. Suspicion of my unannounced arrival was palpable and the small cluster of donga huts and ramshackle buildings rising from the mud had something seething to it. There were plenty of oysters, and oyster shell grit cut tough into the ground everywhere making it knife sharp. But the oysters, like their river, were amazing.

Ado looked down river. I followed his gaze.

"What kinds of fish do you catch?"

"From the river? Right now? – none. They're contaminated. Can't eat them."

"From all that rain and storm churn?"

"Nah, fire retardant".

"Fire retardant?"

A wave of dread hit me. Ado was more philosophical.

"Yeah, it was dumped around a lot of places upstream last year. With the wash off, fish upstream were contaminated straight away but now it's been detected in fish right through here all the way to the river mouth. So, we don't touch them. It'll take time. We don't know how long."

I remembered. On a late afternoon in Spring last year, an out of control fire front was reported burning near Nowra. The whole state was in one of the worst droughts for a century and this fire was a nerve-wracking early sign of an explosive fire season ahead. A social media feed and a phone App alerted me to it. The evening flow of information had said that to control the fire, it was taking over a hundred firefighters on the ground, supported by aircraft, including a newly arrived large Air Tanker called Thor. I remembered thinking at the time how strange it was to use the name of the mythical Germanic God for thunder, lightning, and storms for a water bomb aircraft, when storms caused so many fires. Then I remembered reading that "Thor could drop more than 15,000 litres of water or fire retardant on a blaze within a few seconds." It had super hero status in the State's firefighting artillery. I shuddered.

I swivelled my foot deeper into the sand's cool and watched the grains of sand on the surface slide…"Yeah…it'll probably take quite a while."

"But now they're wanting us to work with them on our traditional cool burning and that's pretty exciting."

I'd heard about cool burning. One had taken place recently where I lived 1000 kilometres south of Nowra. Members of the Dja Dja Wurrung aboriginal clan were working together with State Fire units to understand how preventative burning could save lives and Country using ancient practice and new technology. A local photographer friend had been assigned to document the burn. She returned elated.

"I was here for the cool burn on the farm just a couple of months ago. Five hundred of us mob from across the country getting together to share knowledge. It was awesome. No need to dump that fire retardant here anymore."

From down river, a couple of large water birds skimmed and tilted just above the water surface towards us in a play of aerodynamics and speed. In tandem, they flashed passed continuing up stream. I followed their flight as did Ado. And then a fish somersaulted out of the water and flipped back in with a splash.

"Wow! Happy fish, beat the birds!"

"Hah - yeah, grabbing some grub, probably a black fish – waagu".

The river fell quiet.

"What's the Dharrawal word for this river?"

"Bangalee. It's a water carrier made from bark or wood. We scooped water up into it. The ends of the bark are tied so it's like a bowl. So, in our story we say Country here along the river is a water carrier. Abundance."

"Bangala?"

"Bangalee"

"Bangalee." I repeated under my breath hoping that being here on the banks of Bangalee and imagining it as a brimming bowl would mean I'd hold onto its music.

In the car from Sydney airport, my research friends who'd arrived from Melbourne, Malaysia and the Philippines had fun repeating the names of places as we drove down the coastline towards Bangalee and Bundanon Farm. The town names became a musical countdown to our arrival. Woolongong, Budaroo, Jamberoo, Gerringong, Bombaderry.

"Bundaroo! Jamberoo! Like kangaroo!"

On the way into the Farm where Ado met us, we'd passed road signs to Bangalee, Bangalay and Buangla - a prelude to the river and a taste of

Ado's Dhawararal language that he'd share with us on the banks of the Bangalee.

As he swept his arm from left to right and back again Ado said: "You see across there on the other bank, that's Wandi Wandia clan country. And here on this side of the river it's Wodi Wodi, and upstream a bit there's a small sandstone ridge like a bridge that goes across the river. That crossing meant that clans from all the way south and west could meet here on this site, the farm. It's a place of gathering and ceremony. Boys came in as boys and left as men, so its name means 'boys' place' where boyhood was left behind. Boy – bunda, and noon – place of boyhood.

And you see over there on the other side? You can see that under the trees no native grasses are growing. It's because there've been no cool burns and there are years and years of build-up, too many years of eucalypt leaf and bark litter build-up, which stops the local grasses. If there's a wild fire there, the whole place will go up. The white smoke from the cool burn warns the animals, birds and insects; gives them time to clear out from the site, and the smoke also disinfects – it's like a cleaner. Cool burns are how we've looked after country for thousands of years. And then their spot flames clean up all that litter at a low temperature, the grasses return, and things come back into balance. It means there's a food supply – for everything and everyone."

Ado's eyes sparkled with possibility. As a custodian, he was now brimming with shared ancestral knowledge on cool burns; a knowledge that felt urgent and necessary for our country hit by increasingly prolonged droughts and 'fire storms'.

It then dawned on me that I'd been party to a form of cool burn for many years. During pruning season in the vineyard we'd pack vine cuttings into a converted half forty-four-gallon drum and burn them as we pruned. An old practice from France. The white smoke drift across the vineyard was said to cauterise the vines preventing disease. In the early morning Winter sun, the smoke wisps would fold into the rising fog and hover in a finely woven sheet that stretched across the vineyard wrapping it in a protective shroud.

Bahdu (water), Wagonga (beautiful water, blue water) Mūmbar Naandthari Ngia (I sat watching).

On our walk back from the river bank to where Ado was to hold a 'Welcome to Country' ceremony, I learned how to recognize local trees holding water which could be tapped during drought and there was a native 'soap tree' whose leaves when mixed with water became soapy and cleaned skin. Ado shared a Dharawal name for domesticated dingos buried with their companion 'owner' and we repaired a recently built rough-cut bench seat that faced across the farm fields.

We kept walking. It was time for the ceremony.

A 'Welcome to Country' is most often a cleansing using white smoke from the burning leaves of local symbolic trees. Ado had gathered some Cherry Ballart branches. The thick white smoke from their bright foliage was aromatic. The Cherry Ballart also grows in Dja Dja Wurrung Country where I live. Its use in 'Welcome to Country' and cleansing ceremonies draws on the knowledge that the tree is a partial parasite, taking nutrients from its host plant without harming it. It is a powerful metaphor for visitors to Country who are being invited to share the resources of the land while caring for it as if it was their own. It is also a reminder of the importance of cooperation between people if all are to prosper. The mystery of germinating the Cherry Ballart seed has never been solved.

After Ado welcomed us in Dharrawal language, acknowledging his ancestors and inviting our shared respect for Country, we each in turn stepped into the smoke drift and gently drew it toward and over our heads. A scooping of smoke in much the same way as we'd taken our first steps into the river, cupping its water and tipping it onto our skin ahead of a swim.

We were cooled, cleansed, introduced to the Bangalee, and welcomed to Country. In the wisps and drifts of smoke and ceremony on this ancient gathering place in the Dharrawal language lands of the Yuin Nation where clans had come together over thousands of generations, the tendrils for our collective research were intertwining and wrapping around us. We would now walk together and breathe anew through the haze.

AUTHOR'S NOTE:

This story of 'entanglement' happened recently in Australia as part of our research group's residency at Bundanon Trust Farm which brought scientists and artists together in early December 2018. Ado – Adrian Webster, is a proud Yuin-Thunghutti murrin (person derived from murra (fish) showing connection to the ocean as saltwater people). This story is used with Ado's permission.

AUTHOR STATEMENT, JUDE ANDERSON

An evolutionary theory termed 'punctuated equilibria' suggests sudden and significant change (quantum shift) comes about from the periphery. This includes social evolution. Australia's First Nation people, like those of so many countries, remain marginalised and yet their richly entangled reading of ecosystems and relationship with Country (their spiritual and cultural lands) ensured their survival in Australia for over 60,000 years until colonisation. Integrating First Nation peoples' practices into those of the 21st century has the ability to shift historical paradigms and mindsets, and inspire extraordinary social change. My story is an experience of this.

Untitled by © Emma Arnold, emmaarnold.org

THE GREEN LIZARD

by Albert van Wijngaarden

CHAPTER ONE, MANU

When he was a young boy Father Gregory had told Manu that nothing in life was ever easy, and nothing ever fully clear, and that those who believed otherwise should themselves be considered to be the only simple things in the universe. But as Manu lay in his bed following the circles of his ceiling fan he believed few things less than that, especially since it had been Father Gregory who had told him this.

How could the old priest not see? He has lived here all his life. He has seen the tarmac creep its way up the hills and the dams fill up the valleys. Manu clearly remembered how Father Gregory had always spoken gravely about the tragic disappearance of the birds. Why then, now that more trees were felled than ever before, had he today spoken against the only solution that might have saved what still remained of the forest?

Manu glanced at his phone. Three already and still no sleep. He sat up straight, flicked on his bedside lamp, and went over all that was said at the meeting once more, much of which did not make sense to him: all that money offered to preserve this paradise and at such slight sacrifice to the people living in it. But still, almost everybody had voted against the plan. Of course, the big cardamom planters had organized their camp, and they probably had bought many of those votes, but surely the Fathers could not be bought that easily.

All had seemed fine this morning. Father Gregory had greeted Manu with a smile when he had entered the hall. "My lost child, *finally*, you have returned."

"Yes Father, I am home again. And", Manu had added quickly, "I am ready to help."

"Are you now?"

"Yes Father, I have learned many things about nature and the way we can keep it healthy. Much that can be of use to our community and every living thing around us."

"But my child," Father Gregory had replied in a lecturing manner, "you have been away for a long time. And any absence, however brief, easily turns one's mind and soul loose from the things left behind."

Of course, Manu should have come back sooner. "But my mind was always here, with the village."

Father Gregory had remained silent and looked at him intensely. Then, before hurriedly moving away and leaving Manu confused on the doorstep, he had spoken earnestly, "Remember that true understanding never comes at a distance, one has to live in the midst of darkness before one can hope to find illumination in the light."

That had been the sign that all would not be well.

Suddenly, with a brief flicker his bedside lamp went out, and in complete darkness Manu heard the ceiling fan slow down. Outside, the monotonous zooming of the generator, which had been his constant nighttime companion, died away. Manu sighed as he felt the warm air fall over his body like a blanket—life could truly be unbearable here. How many times had he asked his landlord to replace the ancient device that was unable to keep up with the demands of the tenants of the house? With the pre-monsoon heat reaching its peak and all the ACs in the village running through the night the blackouts had become so frequent that one practically lived on backup energy.

It did not take long before the first small drops of sweat formed on his forehead. It surprised him again how poorly he was able to cope with the temperatures. As a kid, he had lived through times like these and had thought nothing of it. He had enjoyed sitting on the bamboo mats on the old front porch when the midday heat had made it impossible to do anything. On days like that, his father had told him stories about their ancestors and the Gods, and Manu had felt a deep sense of belonging to the world around him. Sitting cross-legged on his little mat he had drunk up every word and felt himself to be floating above the forest, looking down, and looking back, one with every tree, every root, in full understanding of everything around. Those stories had first kindled his interest in the study of nature. It was an interest that had grown into a calling for which he had eventually moved to the big city to attend university.

But in his memories the heat had never been this oppressive. Life here had changed, and so had he. In Delhi, he had for the first time felt *conditioned* air, and now it was difficult to live without it. How had he coped then? He had not even had electric lights, let alone fans. Had it really been this warm then too, or were these the first effects of climate change?

Turning to his side he threw an annoyed glance at the AC unit. It was too energy consuming for the small generator outside and therefore it had been silent ever since this afternoon's power cut. The machine had been idle many times before, but today there was something else about it that annoyed Manu; its clean whiteness, like father Gregory's robe, suddenly seemed foul and intrusive. And why should it not? White is so foreign to the never-ending varieties of green of the forest. It is a color that is not even a color but all colors combined, and thereby it might just have been black, pitch black, like the blackness that remained after a forest fire.

Manu angrily turned to his other side so as not to have to look at the cursed thing anymore, leaving a damp patch where he had lain.

His childhood friend Rajeesh had been at the meeting too. Rajeesh now wore suits and had brandished his big and shiny watch whenever he got the chance. Nothing had changed; Rajeesh had always been an open book.

"So, you are back."

"Yes, Rajeesh, I am. Good to see you again."

"I see you came back with them."

"I have, but they are…"

Before Manu could finish his sentence Rajeesh interrupted him, "Why are you on their side, why do you betray us? Are only you allowed to escape this dirt?"

This remark stung Manu as Rajeesh, who had probably been envious of him, was right in saying that Manu had been able to get away. It was true that Manu knew the value of development first-hand. In a way, he was a product of it. But Manu had also learned that progress is not sacred and that it should not come at this high a price. Even Rajeesh could not have failed to notice that the forest had all but disappeared. What would life be worth here without the clamor of nature? Of course, people need to make a living and should be able to provide a better future for their children. But the goal in life should not be to live like the Americans do in the Hollywood movies. Manu had seen how easily his relatives in the city had fallen before the idols of consumption and production and that it had not made any of them happier. What use were their big cars if they had nowhere worthwhile to drive to anymore? The cities with their foul air were lost already, but here it was not too late. Even though encroachment had turned into widespread destruction the machines had not cut away everything yet. And the proposed plans would have at least saved the little pristine patches that still remained. But how to convince Rajeesh and the other villagers of this?

With a growing sense of agitation, he rolled on his back and stared at the ceiling. If only Father Gregory would have been on their side. How could he have spoken against them? Could he have succumbed to the temptations of money? Or had he developed political ambitions, a new vocation, so late in life? Both options would have sounded utterly preposterous to Manu only a day ago, but now he was not so sure.

The air in the room had grown truly stifling. Manu turned again toward the window in a vain hope that he might catch the slightest breeze. But relief did not come. The branches before his window did not move, as if they too were shocked into immobility by Father Gregory's betrayal.

Manu had come back to assist the foreign specialists and help them to get the local people involved in their green dream. But after today that dream had blackened as it was likely that the tarmac trucks would be back next week already.

Father Gregory had completely mobilized public opinion against them. His old mentor had spoken in a fiery voice, "These people come here and tell us what to do. But they are not from here, they do not understand us."

The audience had grumbled affirmatively.

"Has anyone of them spoken to you about your daily struggles?" he had asked. And they had shouted angrily in reply.

"They will never ask you because they care more about the plants and the trees than about you, their fellow human beings. Furthermore, they are only doing what the Americans and Europeans tell them to. They are the henchmen of the white colonizers who have destroyed their nature, and now come to tell the brown man of India to preserve his at all costs so that they themselves might feel as if they are saving the world and then come here on their expensive holidays and marvel at unspoiled paradise. We say no to this! We were colonized once before, and we will not submit a second time!"

It had been a cheap trick, discrediting all their preservation efforts by linking it to the trauma of colonialism, but it had gotten people on their feet, shouting and booing, and hurling insults at the scientists' bench.

He knew he shouldn't have, but at that point Manu had not been able to restrain himself any longer. He had burst out in disbelief, "What are you talking about? We are on your side!"

Father Gregory had shaken his head as if trying to save Manu from embarrassment. Even though he had heard the audience murmur Manu could no longer keep quiet. "Please understand," he had pleaded, "we cannot go on like this. We need to make real sacrifices. This is not perfect, but we have to be radical! We cannot afford to keep talking anymore; the forest is almost gone. And we cannot do this on our own, we need help; we need their money and expertise."

At that last point, a sea of boos and hisses had engulfed him, and he had felt his powers slip away. In a last despairing effort he had cried out, "Nature is on the verge of surrender, and you still want a bigger piece of it for yourselves," before slumping back into his seat, stunned and shattered, in complete disbelief.

Manu dwelled in his desperation; what could he do? Now nobody would want to work with him anymore.

And then this damned heat!

Turning again to his other side, slick with sweat flowing across his back, his eye was caught by a small lizard that was making its way across the ceiling. It was bright green, and its yellow eyes darted inquisitively round the room following the twitching motions of its body. In small spurts, it moved forward pausing for a little while and then running on again as if chased by some evil spirit.

Right above Manu, the lizard stopped, drooped its head, and looked straight down as if it wanted to speak to him. As it hung there, staring, Manu felt a wave of relief come over him. Maybe not all was lost. Nature grows and lives inside houses too. Maybe it can adjust, adapt, and grow again? The lizard blinked and Manu felt the urge to pour out all that he had withheld at the meeting knowing somehow that the lizard would understand. But just as he opened his mouth to speak the lamp started to flicker, and the ceiling fan spun into action, again startling the little creature and making it jolt across to the window. Reaching the corner, with a final twitch of its tail, it climbed out and disappeared into the night.

Manu stared after it for a while and then felt his gaze drawn toward the map of the Western Ghats he had hung up next to the window. It showed the geology and density of forests and ecological diversity of this region. With a big yellow dot he had highlighted the area that was to be declared protected forest. It was the first thing he had hung up, but something had changed. He blinked and twisted his head. But no matter how he looked Manu could not get rid of the image: that area which man had called Western Ghats, that long green strip of nature running down the entire west coast of India, had on his map gotten a yellow eye and was now like a long green lizard lying there along the length of the continent basking in the heat of the Arabian Sea.

He stared at the map for a long time and then, feeling his eyes growing tired, lay back on his pillow. It was already past four in the morning, and he still had not slept.

CHAPTER TWO, FATHER GREGORY

The calm sea suddenly turned violent, and he hastily waded back to land. He looked frantically about him, but could not find the tree on which he had hung his robe. The thick green of the forest had disappeared. Before him the beach stretched out into the distance like a never-ending desert in which nothing but yellow and brown dust remained. He stepped out into the vast, sandy emptiness. But just as it seemed to him as if he would dwell there forever, suddenly, not too far away a white building with a tall tower appeared. It was his church, and they had already started with the singing of the psalms. Hurriedly, he ran up the steps. But as he drew open the familiar wooden doors he found nobody inside. The singing had stopped, and there was silence, only occasionally interrupted by a splashing sound from a bowl standing on the altar, all the way in the back. Slowly he made his way across the white marble floor. He looked down into the bowl, and saw a green lizard splashing around in murky water fighting for its life. Dismayed, he cupped his hands wanting to save the poor creature from drowning. But as he lifted his hands back up, to his great horror, the animal dissolved in the water and slipped like thick green slime through his fingers.

Father Gregory jolted and gasped for air, streams of sweat dripping down his long brows. He sat up straight, panting—*by God, these hot nights are enough to make a man go mad*, he thought. He tried to switch on the bedside lamp, but it would not work. Stepping out of bed he pulled back a drawer from his desk, scuffled around in it until he finally found an unused match, and lit the long candle standing always ready on his desk. His face was illuminated by the steadying flame as he sat down slowly in his chair.

Resting his heavy head on his fists he looked out of the window over the black valley below. During these power outages, when there were no lights that gave away any sign of human presence, one could imagine oneself as in the old days—surrounded by nothing but nature.

Sipping from a glass of water his mind grew steadily clearer and he felt his dream slip away from him. It had been an eventful day, and then the heat; it was no wonder that the mind would come up with these kinds of vivid spectacles. Drawing in a couple of deep breaths, and filling his lungs with hot air, he went through the notes of the day's events lying before him. Despite the overall success, he had fallen asleep feeling oppressed and burdened by a sense of guilt. An uneasy feeling had nestled inside him at the look on young Manu's face. It had struck him harder than the angry words said by the other scientists. Anger is mere opposition, uncritical, destructive, and therefore easy to dismiss. But genuine disappointment is much more subtle, especially as he knew Manu had not meant to do ill. Maybe it was best to seek him out tomorrow and try to explain things to him in person. Manu would surely understand, it was just that he had been away too long. This had distanced him from reality, and filled his mind with concern for an abstract idea of nature devoid of human presence, wild and untouched. But this nature of his was nothing more than a modern fiction. God had created nature for man to use. And although misuse of nature should always be avoided, he thought, we should never choose soulless plants or animals over human beings.

Obviously, it must have been sad for Manu to discover that the land of his childhood had changed so much. But change had come here long ago already; at first gradually, but now rapidly improving people's lives. Manu only saw the absence of trees, whereas he failed to notice the human gains: now farmers could use tractors and save their spines from bending, children did not have to walk for miles to schools without books, and the ill did not need to rely on witchcraft anymore, but could be cured at hospitals by doctors trained in modern medicine.

He had had to explain it to so many city dwellers before already. From the safety of their concrete jungle they confused the real jungle with an idyllic image of nature. But the real jungle is harsh and unforgiving, and those who live amongst it have the right to improve their lot like everyone else. Manu, too, focused on destruction and did not see that change was also emancipatory. Change had lifted so many up from their role as mere laboring and suffering machines in human form and was allowing them to live life like human should: full of hopes, dreams and faith. Father Gregory lifted his slender index finger as he was accustomed to doing when making an important point during his sermons, and, trying to console his spirit, mumbled out loud: "to Manu most of all the value of progress should be clear." Did the young boy not realize that it had been this change that had enabled him to continue his studies in the city?

And still, no matter how he was able to rationally defend his position, Father Gregory felt ill at ease with his thoughts. He dabbed his sweaty forehead with a towel. What a horrid heat. The monsoon has never been more welcome. With each passing year the temperatures were becoming more unbearable. He thought back on his dream. Could it have been another vision? What if everything would really turn into a desert? Could all this life around him dissolve and slip through his fingers?

He shrugged. No, that was nonsense. He was not against conservation. The scientists had scolded him for preaching the destruction of the forest calling him an enemy of nature. Hah, if they would come to his parish they would see for themselves how much he cared about nature. Had he not developed a system to help farmers switch to more sustainable ways of growing crops? Had he not tried to bring diversity and convert monoculture plantations into oases of biodiversity, that most holy grail of conservationists? Had he not spoken out against the cardamom planters who wanted to cultivate the sacred groves in the valley?

But they did not want to see this. All they cared for were the graphs of species per square mile. Therefore, they advocated the eradication of man from the hills, and from the villages where their ancestors had lived in for centuries; all so that the frogs might return. They were not concerned with preservation, but rather with the delusionary idea of re-naturalization. Of course, we could have used the foreign money, but accepting it would have meant agreeing to their conditions. That would have made people into unwanted elements within protected areas; it would have meant mass relocation, tearing down homes that had stood there for generations. If it had to come at that price, what then would have been the value of this nature? That kind of nature would be nothing more than the commodity of the far away rich, the obsession of scientists and foreigners, who only cared about the idea of a forest and dreamt about harmoniously singing Jungle Book monkeys.

Having worked himself up to a state of utmost excitement he stood up and found himself speaking out loud: "Nature is important, but humanity and the relief of human suffering should always have our priority!" Surprised by his own excitement and looking wearily about him, as if there could have been somebody who had seen his outburst, he quickly sat down again. As he once more returned to his original position and supported his head with his fists the power briefly returned in the village below. For a second or two the valley was illuminated brightly. His eyes, which had grown accustomed to the darkness, could not cope with the light, and he squeezed them to near shut, making the valley below melt away in a bright blurriness. To his horror, he felt as if he had returned to his dream and was standing on that never-ending beach again, and wondering where all the trees had gone. Father Gregory trembled when the lights went off anew. As the comfort of darkness fell over him he quickly folded his hands and prayed to God to give him the strength to make this balance between nature and humanity work.

Chapter Three: Ajith

Down in the valley below the power cut had also awakened Ajith. He lay silently for a while staring up at the holes in the thatched roof above, and accustoming his eyes to the darkness. Maybe it was good the rains had not come yet, for the reed surely would not hold. He stretched his legs and drew a couple of deep breaths. The air was thick with the odors of sweat and hay. Moving nimbly, feeling the way before him like a blind man, he made his way through the maze of entangled arms and legs of his sleeping relatives who lay spread out over the floor of the hut. Upon reaching the front door, he put a cloth round his waist, took his slippers, and went silently out.

It felt good to be outside; the air was still hot, but at least the stink was gone. Kicking some of the plastic bags out of his way that had been torn open by the dogs during the night, he walked up to the well and splashed some water on his face. Not too much, for he knew he would need every drop of it if the rains continued to stay away. He looked about him. Despite the surrounding blackness he could clearly make out the yellow outlines of his crop. It was probably too late already, but he could still try and go to the temple and pray to the Gods that the monsoon might come soon. With the lights off there was nothing to do before sunrise in any case. So, after drying his face, he let the bucket slide back down its dusty trail into the well and started up the hill.

It was a steep walk, and it did not come easy to Ajith, who felt tired, his worries having kept him awake for most of the night. If the harvest would fail again he would probably have no other choice than to follow the others and move away to the city too. Last year's investments had required all of his savings, and the bank wanted its first repayment next month. He should not have gambled like this, and felt sorry for his family that he had let himself be drawn so easily into a dream that had not even been his. What did he care about money? Why had he thought he needed a new fridge, let alone a car? His old life had been filled with poverty and toiling work, but at least he had known what he had, and his family had been happy.

But everybody had been so full of talk about things and how life would be better and easier if only you replaced the old with the new. He had not understood much of it all. But, he had thought, if so many people said it was so, then it was probably the right thing to do. So, he had cut down the trees and in their stead planted the seeds of plants that had never grown in this soil before. He had disturbed the natural harmony and had brought his family on the verge of ruin. If only the Gods would forgive him and let the rains come.

Upon reaching the old tree that looked like a crane he took a sharp right and followed the well-known path up to the temple. In all his life he had never been up here this early, and in the darkness the big trees seemed to tower even higher around him, as symbols of a lost eternity. He touched the largest one of them and bowed his head, feeling tiny and insignificant beside it. Were these the trees about which the man had spoken at yesterday's meeting? He had said they were older than the temple itself and they were essential for every living thing around them.

Everything is connected, of course Ajith knew that, but he had always seen it as a spiritual connection, not something that could affect existence around him during this life. What role in the system had the trees he had cut down played? How much life had he disturbed? The man at the meeting had warned that the forest might disappear if they continued this way. Could that really be possible?

No, of course not, he thought, shaking his head as he quickly stepped on. In his haste to get going he kicked a stone that rolled down the path and crashed into the depths below, awakening a flock of birds whose panicked screeching sounded so ominous that Ajith instinctively bowed deeply.

He had become an intruder on his native soil, continuously disturbing the sacred harmony with every move he made. Feeling a heavy force weighing him down he dipped his head ever deeper as he moved along; making him resemble the old village hunchback by the time he had made his way to the temple entrance.

Carefully removing his slippers, not yet daring to lift his eyes, he climbed up the worn-down granite temple steps. With every step the rank but sweet smell of incense and yesterday's flowers, which had been wedded together by the heat of the night, grew stronger and more potent until, upon reaching the top, he felt completely immersed in it as if he were bathing in a fragrant bath. Slowly, he lifted his head again. Despite the darkness his eyes could clearly make out the familiar coloring on the walls, and he could even see the faint flickering of the statues that were perched away in the niches on the other side of the hall. It had been right of him come here this morning. Steadily regaining confidence he reached up with his right arm and clanged the bell. The clear sound broke the silence in the temple and in his heart. He took a deep breath, clasped his hands together and bowed the bow of ages. Feeling the weight of guilt slowly being lifted from his shoulders he walked toward the golden idols of the Gods, knelt, and prayed to them. He was no longer alone, they were with him, and he felt his worries disappear: things would work out in the end.

He sat there for a while meditating on man's place in the world, until he noticed that behind him the blackness gradually started to give way. It was time for him to go. Soon his family would wake and he had plenty of preparations to take care of as rain would now surely come soon.

Moving backwards, he halted under the brightly painted portal that arched over the temple entrance. As he had done so many times before, he looked up into the yellow eyes of the green lizard that guarded the temple from above. The day's first rays made it look especially vivid, almost alive, and for a second Ajith thought he saw it move. He nodded solemnly to the creature, turned his back toward the temple, walked down the steps, and made his way back down into the valley below.

AUTHOR STATEMENT, ALBERT VAN WIJNGAARDEN

This story is based on real conversations I had with people involved in the rejected India High Range Landscape Project in the southernmost regions of India's Western Ghats. I found that all parties had valid arguments, but failed to communicate with one another. This story therefore aims to humanize individual narratives that are entangled through complex social and economic realities, and to convey the importance of attempts at mutual understanding to further positive change.

The Park from the series, Presence of Things Unseen
by © Siri Ekker Svendsen, siriekker.com

THE VISITOR

by Julia Naime Sánchez-Henkel

This morning, as I heard your boat approaching the riverbank, I instinctively got scared. The sound of a boat is a usually a warning call, an omen of sorrow and despair to our home. As your boat approached, those who could ran away into the forest. I, rooted to the spot, stayed attentive and observed, trying to carefully track your movements. I expected the worst. But the white and green hummingbird that likes to visit my flowers every morning told me you were alone and unarmed. While I felt relieved, I still don't know for what reason or purpose you have come. Before you do or say anything, I want to introduce you to our home. You see, you have arrived to a very special place: the Amazon rainforest.

To a visitor like yourself, our home might seem eerie and daunting. Indeed, when you are not well acquainted with your surroundings, any environment can quickly become uninviting. I hope that I can persuade you to think otherwise and convince you that I live in a beautiful home. It is a home teeming with life, lush and vibrant; it beholds life like no other place on Earth.

Seen from the river where you came from, the rainforest looks as still as a wall. The riverine trees prevented you from seeing anything behind their leafy curtain. As you came closer to the tangled wall, you realized that you were not approaching still life, quite the contrary: an insect's orchestra welcomed you, playing you a loud symphony of dissonant sounds. Get used to them. Insects are the rainforest's background music. They provide the tempo to which all other life forms dance. Their clamorous welcome is the indicator of the thriving diversity you will find once you enter the rainforest. Did you feel excited, or intimidated?

When you arrived to the riverbank, I noticed how you got off your boat, placed your feet on the roots of the tree that is holding on tightly to the sandy soils, and took a big step to enter the rainforest. You looked so tired, after spending so much time under the merciless sun. As you entered the rainforest, a fleet of mosquitoes welcomed you; apologies if they made you feel a bit uneasy. Any attempt at scaring them away is futile; I recommend you accept defeat before you start the war. They condense here for the same reason as you: they are terrified of the burning sunlight and the crushing heat. Keep walking and you will soon forget about them.

Now that you are grounded under the canopy of trees, I will unveil to you the mysteries and wonders of my world. But first, give your spirit some time to surpass the sensation of diminishment, as you stand under the elevated tree crowns. Trees are imposing, magnificent beings under whose crowns you might feel insignificant. A greenish foreground dominates your vision, contrasting the vast blue sky you could see while still on the river. Give your eyes some time to adjust to the monochrome spectacle. Shrubs, palms, animals and trees are densely overlapping each other. In the most diverse factory of life on Earth, everything that your eye can see is relatively close to you; there is no horizon.

While the rainforest might seem at first a confusing, labyrinthine chaos, for the trained and attentive mind it as an ordered amalgam of life. You might think that the world I am about to show you is fictional; indeed, it is almost magical. But rest assured it is as real as the palms of your hands. In the rainforest, I can prove to you that the wonders of the world are not necessarily novelties; there are often hidden jewels in the most familiar, the most ordinary. Nature becomes fantastical when you give yourself the time to explore it. Attention, properly applied to anything, will reveal to you marvels. I hope that the guided visit to our home will trigger in you a firm sense of wonder and humility.

During your visit, I beg you to be silent and respectful, so you can see everything that I want to show you. You will find that it is quite easy to walk among the rainforest's trees. With their shade, the highest trees control what grows in the soil, creating natural and winding paths. These trees are like an army of soldiers, governing and supervising the never-ending terrestrial unrest. Many plants below them are patiently waiting to take over their privileged position closer to the sun. Some trees take any opportunity to thrive; they live fast and die young. Others are more prudent, growing slowly but surely. Look at the forest floor: the youngest seedlings are developing new leaves next to some sterile looking mushrooms. Do not let appearances fool you, mushrooms might seem innocuous, but they are of paramount significance. They are the messengers of the rainforest. It is through them that trees communicate between each other, and it is through them that I know about your movements.

The soil on which you are standing is an accumulation of vegetable and animal debris. Living in the soil is a delicate mesh of small and microscopic—yet essential—beings who are continuously working to recycle everything we leave behind. All the life that is surrounding you takes its energy and nutrients from that thin layer of decomposing waste. Out of death, new life is constantly arising. Which reminds me: when walking through the rainforest always be careful where you step; you might hurt something. Or, something might hurt you. You do not want to step on the tiny but mighty coral snake—very small compared to the infamous anaconda—whose venomous bite could promptly kill you.

As you walk, imagine that you are walking on the greatest cathedral ever built. Realize that the rainforest and its trees are offering you monumental, awe-inspiring beauty to which you can claim no authorship; it is a beauty produced by chance and time alone. Consider it as an architectural masterpiece constructed by thousands of years of evolution, far transcending any cathedral that humans have, or will ever, build. Observe the details of the green dome that is shielding and protecting you from the sun. Gaze at the beams of light that are piercing the verdant ceiling of the cathedral, illuminating the rich world around you. Do you notice the two blue butterflies that are gently flying from one wooden column to another? You are witnessing majesty, you are literally surrounded by it.

Keep walking until you cross a small stream. To this area often comes a brocket deer with its cub, to eat the leaves of the thorny bushes. The little cub is a voracious eater. I always see him avidly jumping around tasting new leaves. If you come here at night, you might also see a female tapir playing in the water with her big nose and getting her feet wet. Oh, look! A few meters to your left, there is an agoutis—the small rodent next to the trunk of the *Huayruro* tree—digging a hole to hide the nuts it has collected. It's a greedy little beast! They spend a lot of time carefully accumulating and storing their food. They seem to be constantly worried about something bad happening to them, they are anxious and nervous.

Now, go a bit deeper into the rainforest until you spot the tree trunk with a white shiny bark, then, turn to your right. That tree is called *Cecropia*. Don't climb it! An army of zealous ants lives in the tree's trunk, and they will feverishly defend it from any intruder. There is, however, one animal that spends most of its life in the tree and makes a feast out of the ants. I am talking about the serene, dopey-faced sloth. The sloth is the opposite of the agoutis; it is the most relaxed, laziest animal of the rainforest. I enjoy his calm, laid back attitude. He moves so slowly that even his eye blink can last more than a second. Wait… It seems he is turning his head around, he must be curious to see your face. Let's wait… Just a little bit more…. Now, finally! You can stare into his eyes. As your eyes meet, don't you have the sensation that the creature has already formed a special relationship with you, with its drowsy, almost lovesick, expression on its face? Part of the thrill of being in the rainforest is the feeling of being recognized and accepted. Here, we accept all kinds of life. The vicious, the slow, the greedy, the venomous, and even the dopey ones. We all have a role to play.

Keep going on and be sure to walk between the young *Kopak* tree—with its bulky and woody thorns covering its trunk—and the palm tree. While the trunk of the *Kopak* tree is harmless, be careful not to touch the trunk of the palm tree, with its long, pointy and venomous spines. Walk straight for a couple more meters and you will soon spot a tree trunk that is not one, nor two, nor three, but four meters wide! It also has buttress roots two meters high. It should inevitably catch your eye as it is one of the greatest natural monuments that the rainforest can offer you. It might even take your breath away. That splendid, spectacular, glorious, elegant tree…. is me. Come closer, so I can tell you more about this forest and my story.

My name is Manshika, but humans call me *Shihuahuaco*. I am one of the thickest trees that you will see in the rainforest. While I am not as tall as my brother the *Kopak* tree, whose crown can be as high as 60 meters and his trunk three meters wide, I am sturdier and heftier. My buttress roots extend as far as four or five meters beyond my trunk. Look up and you will see my crown, rising high into the sky. Be careful not to feel dizzy as you try to find my highest branch, more than 30 meters above your head. From the tips of my roots to my highest leaf, I am filled with life. Your eyes can't see all the marvels that I hide from my roots to the crown. I will walk you through them.

First, take some time to walk around my trunk. See how high and long my buttress roots are? They serve as fences, providing an enclosed environment for some animals. During the rainy season, the soil gets flooded and many fish lay their eggs between my roots, I keep them protected from the currents. I am sort of the godfather of many of these creatures; through the years, I have watched over entire lineages of fish families.

While you were walking all around my trunk, did you notice the small entrance to a cave inside me? The cave formed because as I grew, I had to give up my oldest cells. I had to economize my resources; I am quite a gluttonous tree! To enter the cave, you have to get on your knees and crawl. As you kneel, embrace the smell of the humid earth and decomposing litterfall permeating the air. It has a unique freshness, don't you think? Once you are inside, you will be able to stand: it is a cave at least two meters high. Inside the cave, you will see two bats, sleeping upside down. These two fellows are archetypal party animals; they always go out late at night and come back at daylight to sleep practically all day!

Leave my cave to go outside again. A meter above your head, you can see a group of carved, parallel lines on my bark. These are the prints of a male jaguar, who was here yesterday, scratching his nails, marking his territory. The jaguar is a solitary and taciturn animal; he does not like sharing his space or time with others. He is always walking solemnly in the rainforest, absorbed in his own thoughts, protecting us. I like when he visits me because he shares what he has seen on his prowls. He has chosen to remain invisible to your eyes; but he knows you are here. Isn't that somewhat thrilling? In the rainforest, it is hard to know who is watching you - especially if you are a visitor.

Above the jaguar's traces, you will see a thick woody liana horizontally crossing my trunk. Look attentively so you don't confuse the green iguana that is on it with a leaf. They camouflage to fool the snakes and hawks that feed on them. Things are not always what they seem, nature demands scrutiny. Further up, in my branches, you might see some colourful, cone shaped plants, the *Bromeliads*. A *Bromeliad* plant can store as much as three liters of water between its leaves. It is a breeding ground for many frogs, and a source of water for monkeys and other tree climbing mammals. *Bromeliads* establish their roots in trees like myself, to steal my sap and feed themselves. I do not mind it that much as their presence helps me attract monkeys and other gregarious animals that disperse my seeds.

Speaking of monkeys… are those…? Unbelievable! There is a family of yellow-tailed monkeys jumping playfully between my branches. Can you see them? They are very rare to see. You are very lucky! Nature gives wonderful surprises. After all these years, I still get excited when they visit me; they are so joyful! They heard you coming, and they were curious to see who you are. I have told them that they should not be afraid of you, since you are harmless…. right?

Start looking down again now, towards my roots. In my lowest branch, you can observe the aerial roots of a strangler fig tree, suspended in the air. This tree is the most rebellious tree of all, a strong dissident of our rules and customs. It spends its first years not growing up to reach the sky but growing down to reach the soil. Talk about a revolution! While it grows to reach the ground, it gets all its nutrients from my sap. This tree might be my future killer: its roots will slowly and gently strangle me on their way to the ground. You might think: "How ungrateful, he nurtures him, and this is how he thanks him."

Don't worry. This is how life works in the rainforest; I know the role I have to play in it. When I was young, I had to fight for survival. I feared being stepped on by a tapir, eaten by a deer, or blighted by a fungus. Growing up, I faced the harsh competition for sun and light with other trees. I survived not because I was stronger, but because I was luckier. I survived because many others died. Now, as I grow older, fatter, taller, I have realized that my existence—or for that matter, anyone's existence—is just the consequence of fortunate events. I give back what chance and life have given me by hosting other species, helping others thrive. It is my purpose, my responsibility. I accept that one day it will be my time to leave. After all, we are all part of nature, and we are made in such a way that we can survive only with the help of other species.

At this point, your curious and hopefully mesmerized mind might be wondering why am I sharing this with you and why am I taking so much time to describe the diversity that I love and cherish. You see, the life that surrounds us is neither static nor perpetual. It has been shaped by time and life alone, ever since my ancestors started working the soils and providing a microclimate for the many species to thrive. Before us trees, the Amazon was a deserted basin filled with sand. My ancestors, like diligent and relentless farmers, worked on these lands for thousands of years to bring shelter, water, and food to everyone.

In just a couple of years, there have been radical changes in the empire that it has taken us trees thousands of years to build... I have not told you about one very important species of the rainforest, one that frightens me more than the strangler fig, as it is much more powerful and clever. It is your species, the human species. I've heard, seen and felt the sorrow of many of my brothers, sisters, cousins, as they were killed and chopped by humans, and their corpses carried away to an unknown slaughter house. Whenever someone of your species visits us, there is damage to our home, the beautiful temple in which you are standing and to which you also belong. I am probably one of the few old growth trees that your species has left standing, but I do not know for how long I will be this lucky. That is why I was so afraid of you when I heard you coming.

It might be hard to imagine, but you should know that our relationship with humans has not always been this sour. When I was younger, everything was different. Among all the species of the rainforest, the human species impressed me for many reasons, both for its physical abilities as well as its social behaviour. The humans could be agile as a monkey when climbing a tree, light footed and dexterous as a jaguar when hunting, and loud as the howler monkey when they were fighting against each other. They could be greedy as the agoutis, lazy as the sloth, tricky as the iguana, and playful as the tapir in the water. Humans impressed me because they had all types of animals inside them. Humans passed by this area in flocks of 30 to 40, always during the dry season, to be near the many natural ponds filled with fish.

Humans would settle around me and build temporary huts with palm leaves, tying them up with thin lianas. They fed on many different animals of the rainforest. They fished using the wild yam *Barbasco* and crafted many items such as the blowgun, to hunt at a distance. They frequently hunted the small rodent paca, while the luckiest hunted the capibara, the biggest rodent of the rainforest. Another prey they seem to be fond of was the wild pig, such as the collared peccary. Those are tough to catch—the peccary are aggressive animals and always run in a pack. The highest price any hunter could get was to capture the rainforest's only and unique eagle, the harpy eagle. The eagle was never eaten by humans, it was unthinkable. It was a hunter's most valuable possession, to keep as a sign of power and dignity.

Humans of the rainforest also ate numerous plants. I would often see women meticulously collecting a few seeds of selected species, such as the palm of *Aguaje* or the *Ungurahui*. They would plant everything near their settlement, creating wonderful gardens, with up to 80 different species. We were all grateful, as this brought more life and diversity to our home; I had more nutrients to feed on. With them, nature was nurtured.

What seemed even more remarkable to me, is that compared to other species, humans formed very close bonds with other living species. It seemed they understood that every plant and animal has a specific personality, a unique character. I recall that children would gently hold turtles to play with them, widowers or elders would patiently nurture monkeys as if they were their own child, and adults would take care of the many birds with which they sang. Humans loved singing. They sang beautiful lullabies to each other and to other beings of the rainforest, especially when they hunted or gathered. They even adopted many bird songs to communicate.

I learned to recognize some of their signals. The sound of the horned screamer was a warning call when they spotted an enemy, the song of the white owl was used when entering someone's hut, and playful midnight lovers flirted with the song of the plumbous pigeon.

And so it was. Our home, the rainforest, produced the food humans ate, the water they drank, and the medicines with which they cured their diseases. They took from the rainforest what they needed to live. However, the rainforest also took from them. Under the trees, humans lived daily dramas and tragedies: a grandmother eaten by a jaguar, a child poisoned by a viper, a fisherman bitten by a piranha. In the rainforest, uncertainty and insecurity are omnipresent; it is fundamental to learn to accept and adapt to them. Humans seemed to understand this. There is a price to be paid for living a careless life in such bountiful and extravagant nature. I thought this way of life would go on forever, until one day we received new visitors that changed everything permanently, in ways I could not have fathomed. As I was blossoming and laying my first seeds of the year, a new congregation of humans arrived to the rainforest. They had garments covering their bodies and brought with them many extraordinary objects that were not produced in the rainforest. These alien humans came in small groups, ten to twelve. They were all men, no women nor children. They cleared and cut down the rainforest to build up houses and grow plants that I had not seen before.

The alien humans started interacting with the rainforest humans, who seemed completely enchanted by foreign objects. Alien humans brought shiny tools that cut deeper and faster through any animal skin or wood, some small shiny round objects, and wooden figures and cruxes. The rainforest humans began to live with the alien humans, accepting them and almost eager to become like them. Human lives and their behaviour toward all of the members of the rainforest changed progressively. Or, as I look back, should I say, rather dramatically. They forgot how to communicate with us, forgot our characteristics, and how they could use us.

If before humans only fished according to their feeding needs, now they were extracting more fish than what they needed to survive. If before I saw men and women gently gathering and managing forest trees, now adults were painstakingly cutting us down to grow foreign plants for more and more hours. Instead of seeing men hunting the few monkeys that still dare to come to my branches, men hunted jaguars and ocelots, not for their meat, but for their skin. One day I even saw one member of the group give away his highest possession, the harpy eagle, in exchange for a couple of those little, shiny round objects. At that moment, my sap stopped flowing. If they were able to give away their dearest possession, they would never treat their home, the rainforest, and all the living beings in it, the same way. Our relationship with humans had irreversibly changed.

The rainforest has never been the same. I long for the people that I used to live with. I stopped seeing the children coming to play in the rainforest, or the lovers singing lullabies to each other between the trees. We have been forcefully reassigned to a background position in the human landscape. Humans became afraid of the home that provided them with food and shelter for so many years. They became more and more like the anxious agoutis, accumulating objects—those little, round shiny objects— without a clear purpose. It is as if there are no limits to the human's needs and wants from the rainforest. They all want more without giving back anything, and in the process, they are hurting us.

I should ponder on what the humans gained from these changes: they tend to live longer, they have more children, they have more possessions to which I see they hold to dearly. If before they ate once per day, now they eat twice or three times. They do not have to migrate around the forest looking for food; they live in permanent, walled houses raising animals previously unknown to the rainforest. Most importantly, they face less uncertainty. They do not abide by the rainforest rules anymore. Humans chose to create and live in another world, a world where we are no longer considered. However, I wonder: can the human relationship with nature and its diversity be lost without consequences? I fear that there are challenges ahead that will require all the species of the Earth to cooperate. We need you just as you need us.

In recent years, it has become harder and harder for us plants to grow. Indeed, I have felt a lot weaker. I know it is not because I am aging, although I am more than 500 years old. No, it is not that. We are becoming less productive. We have less energy and nutrients to grow. The heat that arrives every summer makes us transpire excessively, there are more fires, and the rainfall has become more intense. Water arrives in greater quantities for shorter periods, making it hard for our roots to absorb it. Moreover, every year, as more trees are cut down, there are less of us that can regulate the weather of the rainforest. We are weaker, and we are fewer.

The changes in weather affect many of us, both plants and animals. It even affects you humans. I have seen how the more frequent flooding destroys your crops and your settlements, how the excessive fishing and the warmer waters are depleting the fish stocks on which you feed. We are all agonizing because of something big and ubiquitous that is weakening all the living beings of the rainforest. By sharing this story, I want to persuade you, to convince you, that you and I are different in form but not in nature. We all breathe the same air, drink the same water, feed on the same molecules.

Maybe one day all the diversity and life that my ancestors and I have worked for thousands of years to build and maintain will no longer be, and you will be surrounded by a manufactured environment. Do you think it is worth destroying the unique and genuine to build something superfluous and artificial? As a species, what empire do you want to create, and in what universe do you want to contemplate and feel mesmerized? If you lose us, what will your heart and soul ponder at when looking for inspirational thoughts or feelings of bewitchment? We are your source of imagination, of creativity. As the stewards of this Earth, are you willing to let that go?

Look at me again. You can see me as still life, a fragile, inanimate tree defenceless against a powerful and intelligent human as yourself. Or, you could recognize that I, and the rainforest that I have showed you, is not only a source of raw materials, it is also, and most importantly, a complex habitat for thousands of species that feel, learn, and think, just like you. You could find in us inspiration, respect, humility, and potential allies. We, all the species of the rainforest, have worked to build an exceptional world filled with transcendental beauty for you to contemplate. We believe that an essential and unique attribute of your species is the capacity to contemplate, to cherish the simplest rock or mineral to the highest and most powerful tree. It is what makes you human, of this I am convinced.

AUTHOR STATEMENT, JULIA NAIME SÁNCHEZ-HENKEL

The Visitor relates to quantum social change in two ways. First, it describes the richness of our world and the connection between living beings from a non-anthropocentric perspective. Second, it emphasizes the relevance and uniqueness of human agency in shaping the future, and aims to empower and inspire.

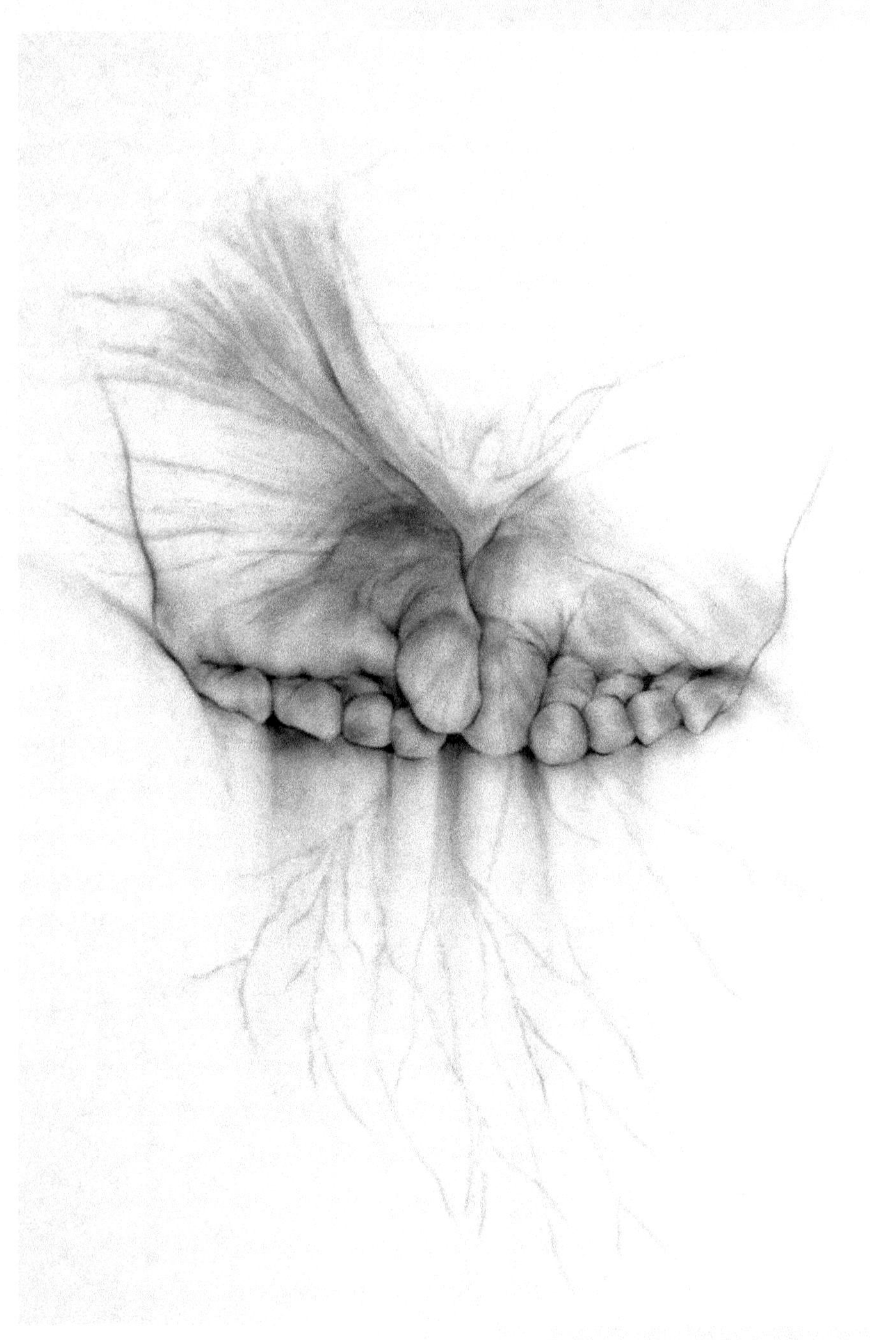

Reverberations IV by © Jill Ho-You, jillhoyou.com

Let Us Begin

by Saher Hasnain

Shaden set her cup on the step beside her and leaned into the wall, then turned her face to the sun and focused her attention on the neighborhood.

Her mother, Rafiqa, sat down on the stairs next to her and waved to the neighbor across the road. "When I was your age, this was impossible."

Her mother's shawl-wrapped head eclipsed the sun. "Loitering in public was not a thing for the respectable woman."

"What's stopping you now?" Shaden asked, taking a careful sip of her tea.

"*Uffff.* I am too old to change my habits. Even in this new environment." Rafiqa laughed and went inside.

Shaden stretched out some more, squinting into the stream of people walking past. People stopped and greeted others enjoying the weather. She let the crowd's relaxed energy tide over her senses. This easily managed communal awareness that grounded her while creating the possibility of exploration was familiar and comforting. Reaching out, she sensed the high-strung energy of apprentices in the processing plant. She grinned and drew back to herself. Coming back to her own consciousness always brought a feeling of deflation and disappointment. Her teacher had called it *decoherence*: the disappointment of separating from the collective.

She drank the rest of the tea and went inside to get her supplies. Picking up her backpack, she looked around for her mother. Her mother was one of the few remaining people in their community who had been unable to complete the training and connect with them. Shaden found her shelling a bowl of peas.

Shaden picked up her goggles and helmet. "I'm off. It's time."

A flicker of dismay flashed across her mother's face. "Already? But it's not until after the festival, *haina?*"

"It is, but I have to finish checking the harvest first."

Rafiqa set the bowl to one side and stood up. "Shaden, don't go. Who knows what will happen with those people?"

"It's simple, *I* will happen to them." The old joke.

Before her mother could speak again, she engulfed her in a hug. Squeezing the frail body toward her for a few breaths, she quickly turned away and left. It was better this way.

The red dust burst out from under her bike and unfurled around her path. Granules of sand flicked up against her face and goggles.

The Potohar spread out its expansive arms for her.

She reached the edge of the plateau and stopped. The sun was lowering itself slowly into the thick blanket of smog over the old cities. Her mother said the smog been a lot worse (and a lot closer) in her days.

Shaden got off her bike and pulled it under the shade of a tree. It was one of last hardy ones that had survived this far inland towards the cities. Slinging her backpack over her shoulders, she headed down the roughly carved pathway on the side of the plateau. Her mentor had helped her carve out the hand holds and rock pockets.

She swung down with the careless ease of familiarity. Dropping off the hill-face at the last few feet, she took off her boots and lined them up next to the concrete block she used as a table.

She put her bag on top of them to protect them from the heat and took stock. Heat baked granules pressed into her feet. The community felt uncomfortably distant. The settlement was over the plateau, more than twenty kilometres behind her. But it *was* there, a foundation for her to hold on to if she needed the comfort and orientation.

She tossed her head back and tied her hair up with her scarf before walking to the hulking landscape of failed and killed buildings from the nearby cities. Her bare feet found purchase on the crumbling blocks of concrete. Scrambling over rusting rods of rebar, she reached the first batch of her lichen. She thrust her hand into the cool clumps in front of her and pulled. Good. Their foundations were excellent, and the algae was doing better than she had expected. The symbiosis with the fungus was holding.

She moved on, jumping over yawning crevices and using the occasional steel beam to vault over to other levels. She was on the lookout for browning clumps of lichen and signs of pests.

She finished her rounds in another two hours and dropped into one of the deeper hollows of the concrete field to find water. No warning signs of algal failure so far. She squeezed a thick clump of the blossoming algae and let the water trickle into her mouth. The algae in the shaded parts of the field was always dripping with condensation.

Soon it would not be safe to sit in these hollows. The lichen was working its way through rapidly and the concrete was starting to crumble. The blistering daytime heat, the monsoons, and the occasional smog overflow did not help matters either. Or did, depending on how one looked at it. Helped along with a productive blanket of lichen, they did not have long to wait for this urban debris to vanish into the original landscape.

She was putting it off and she knew it. Looking around the lush gloom once again, she took to her feet and ran back. If she rushed now, she could make it back for the set-up of the festival.

Everything she did these days had the flavour of goodbyes. She would never see her field again. She would never slice off clumps of lichen to sell to Erfaan again. She would never feel envious about his link to the cities again.

She would never see her mother again, either.

She coaxed another burst of speed from her bike as the tent-tops came into view. The families would be setting up the food tables and cooking. The festival took place on one of the larger table-top formations in the Potohar. Massive tents had been erected overnight, under the responsibility of different families. Her greater family had always taken care of the food. She felt giddy already, the pervasive presences of the hundreds of people moving through the festival grounds was comforting and energizing.

"Shaden! You've been out in the fields!" Her uncle Saad called out to her from his food stall. He was loading it with trays of cooked slices of meat and skewers of vegetables. His son was helping set up chairs and water flasks.

She went up to them and helped herself to a small plate of food. She pulled the contents of the skewer into her mouth. The thin slices of meat were meltingly tender against the fresh crispness of the vegetables. The fat-charred spices glistened on the peppers and pearly onions. It was phenomenal. Uncle Saad had a skill with spices and a deeper connection during cooking than anyone she knew.

"*Alhamdulillah*, everything is doing well. The next farmer will not have any problems."

"*You will never eat this again either,*" she thought sadly.

"This is good news. The Capital Territory is asking for more air scrubbers," her uncle said, clearly pleased.

"What?" Shaden exclaimed."

"But we've already given them twice as many as before this summer!"

"Yes, but it's because they are finally seeing the improvements. Erfaan's new formulation is doing wonders with the smog and they want to start adding it to new locations."

"He's not going to be happy with this, you know," Shaden said, thinking of Erfaan's already over-worked production team.

"*Haan haan,* but when is he ever happy? I can feel him in the back of mind whenever he is near. He is like a mosquito bite rash in my mental map of the community when I connect with him."

Shaden laughed and handed back the empty skewers.

"Visit if you can. You don't have to live your whole life out there," Saad said, tossing the skewers into a tray.

Very sobering. He was right, of course. Shaden felt him as a solid and comforting presence. Why couldn't her mother be like him? The siblings were almost the same age, but Rafiqa had always resisted. She *must* have resisted. The trainers of the process had anticipated that the entanglement would be difficult for the older generations, but there were not many who had been immune to gradual development of the entanglement. Her mother was now one of the rare few left who had not changed at all. It was not biological, otherwise it would have shown up in her too. And she was good enough to be selected for this stage. Saad had cottoned on to the process as though he had been training himself unconsciously his whole life. "I just think of it as sharing in the deeper things that make us people, you see," he had said.

After thanking him for the food and company, Shaden headed off toward the center of the festival. She needed to immerse herself in the energy of the people. It was good to do this as much as possible now before she was driven off into the proper wilderness—the extremely peopled wilderness of the cities that had resulted in the building-graveyard she worked on. There were crowds of people who were content to rub shoulders with those they couldn't – or *wouldn't* -- link with. It was the time of the individual out there; empowerment taken to the outer limits of the spectrum.

The bustling energy of the people setting up stalls, shouting out instructions to family members and calling out greetings wrapped around her. She let herself sink slowly into the awareness of the crowd. The trainers had once called it mind-reading for the soul. Tuning oneself on the same resonance and meaning that lay dormant under all the stresses and drives of an everyday life.

She shook herself. The momentary homesickness agitated her connection.

The people setting up the rug stall on her right looked at her curiously. They had sensed her unease. She smiled at them and moved on, spreading herself thinner and thinner into the mass of humanity on the festival grounds.

"Shaden, here!" Idhaar, her main trainer, waved at her from the central tent. She shook off the warm near-somnolence of the entanglement and went to him.

"This is a big day for us, *haina?*" He looked down at her, eyes twinkling in the firelight.

"I am hesitant." Shaden fidgeted nervously with the straps of her bag.

"You never were one for many words. Being nervous is fine. It is good. You understand the gravity."

They went inside. Two other trainers had arrived and were unpacking their bikes.

This part of the festival would be confined to the trainers and the students. They would convene for the task and then rejoin the festival. It was highly probable that this was the last time she would be here.

"You are always so negative! You shouldn't be. Being negative gives you wrinkles."

Uff! Would she always have Rafiqa's voice in the back of her mind? She absently rubbed the space between her eyebrows to flatten out the frown lines there.

The rugs were set up and the students had arrived. The tent dwarfed the small group of people. One trainer to a student. Each pair held a map spread out in front of them. Everyone had divested themselves of their belongings near the door.

"You have heard this many times from me now. But you need to have this hammered in. Nobody has done this before at such scale." Amreen, the facilitator, looked at the pairs in the room. Already a tall woman, she towered over the seated students.

Shaden looked closely at the deep lines slashed between Amreen's eyebrows and bracketing her mouth. The long dark hair coiled over her shoulder was generously shot through with grey. The last few years of refining the process and training the teams had worn her thin. She was one of the pioneering five who had started the process two decades ago. She was their de facto leader.

"Our reasons remain the same. The world is more complex than ever before. We need more ways of working together, of harnessing the power of human nature to solve our bigger problems. We needed to go bigger than those small incremental solutions that were the norm when I was young and that persisted into your youth. Recycle. Go plastic-free. Eat vegan. But this is not enough."

The trainers placed small white stones on the maps at specific points as she spoke. It was where each of them would be stationed.

"In my day, the closest we got to entanglement and connection was through the Internet, or through group religious activity. That last one was declining quite quickly even then!"

Khareem, one of the trainers, muffled a laugh. His father was one of the last remaining religious scholars in the region.

Amreen walked around the room, pausing briefly behind each student. "I remember a day when my sister and I were out in a market. We were standing at a stall, looking at shirts, I think. We were very engrossed." She was coming closer. Shaden's skin prickled.

"I only noticed the man when he was right behind me." Amreen's voice was directly behind her head. "You wouldn't understand this, of course. And this shows me how far we've come. Latif will tell you about the neuroscience of all this, but what I felt was a *presence*. A looming, dangerous presence that made me snap my head back and break his nose as he was leaning in to smell my hair."

Shaden was surprised. The very concept of someone being able to *sneak* up on someone was alien to all the students in the room. They would have been aware of the person even if they were not participating in the entanglement.

Amreen walked out in front of them and turned to face them. "Women in our country have always been viscerally aware of their surroundings. Far more aware than men have had to be. We can *feel* eyes on us. We can *feel* when dangerous people, *men,* are around. Of course, this applies to other people in the rest of the world. My sister and I wondered how we could use this visceral awareness. If at all."

Someone entered the tent. Amreen looked at the visitor and beckoned him towards her. "Latif was working on solving our pollution issues. He discovered that there was no difference between getting governments and corporations to change habits, and individual people to change habits. It seemed like humanity was the problem, but the only way to do something was to target humanity through its individual components."

Professor Latif stepped carefully through the sitting pairs and looked at each one with great pleasure. A thin and spare man, his face was a skull papered with greying skin. His battle with vaccine-resistant TB had hounded him throughout his entire life. His deathly angularity was a terrible thing to behold – especially in contrast with his bright and loud personality.

"I am very pleased with how we started it all. We honestly didn't think we would have to rely on the same process to spread the connection. But there you are!" Latif looked at the group and sighed deeply. "Your work will be difficult. We can't make your way easier. We can't do anything except teach you from our experience." He sat down in the center of the room.

"As seeds of connection, you are to plant this awareness and connection into the people you will meet. It is the same way you learned. But instead of your communities, who were working together to nurture this, you are going into a world that has been carefully growing its ideas of individuality and personal presence. They do not know what we have been working on."

Shaden sat up straighter. She felt the nervousness radiate from Arfaat, the youngest student in the group. Arfaat was the only one to have been born into their community as it was learning communal entanglement. He had always lived with the background hum of the community, and had never known a life of isolated mental individualism. Shaden and the others still remembered their childhood, when adults gently taught them how to develop their connections with the others.

Professor Latif continued. "Our little experiments here and in Baltistan have shown that this works. Of course, that was easier, as we were working with those who *wanted* this to succeed. The only way now is to spread. Our goals are still the same. We need collaboration and community to solve the problems around us. We have shown that together our creative problem solving is greater. We have transcended the petty individual ambitions that hold us back as a people."

Shaden felt a bloom of pride at the thought of their air-scrubbing ventures and their communal use of resources.

He smiled. "This is the brink of something wonderful. You have experienced how natural our connection feels. And, it will get deeper and more meaningful, the more we do it. We have found the way of pulling free from limitations of selfish personhood. We can harness the great power of community. We have done this here. There is no need for the great convulsion and chaos of a revolution or an apocalypse. We have shown that there is a better way. A gentler way."

Amreen locked eyes with her briefly. "*But it didn't work with my mother.*"

"Let us begin." Shaden said quietly.

The noise of the festival faded to a dull drone. The trainers started with their regimen.

They were lying down behind the tent. The training was over. They were recovering. She could see Arfaat's foot at one edge of her vision, and Sameena's head at the other, with her arm thrown over her eyes. The ground stabilized their overwrought awareness. It was immense and comforting under them.

She started to spread herself out, touching the presence of her fellow students and reaching into the festival. The bright and energetic nodes of the participating people calmed her down. There were a few people like her mother. Dark points that you could not interact with. But they were few and far between.

Arfaat let out a trembling sigh. "It is going to be so lonely and quiet."

Shaden brought herself back. "*Cht.* We are going in to one of the most crowded cities. The noise of the shrieking individual presences will be deafening."

"You know what I mean! It will be as if we are surrounded by the silence of the black holes!"

Sameena gasped and sat up, looking nervously at Shaden.

Black holes. The non-participants. The ones you could throw encouraging nudges at through the community convergence and get nothing back. All feedback streams ended with them. It did not matter how badly they wanted to be part of it - they took everything and gave nothing back. Her mother was a black hole.

"Sorry Shaden. You know what I meant…"

"*Haan haan*. Forget it. We can do this. We are the best option so far." Shaden tried to convince herself.

"But won't we be making them do something they don't want to?" Hamza asked. He was Latif's grandson. He had been born in Kabul, the biggest urban conurbation in the northwest now. He would return to his mother's family for his placement.

"Every human craves connection. They show this with their hundreds of online friendships and desires for validation from people they've never met. Our nudges won't force anything. They will just nurture the unconscious desire to develop deeper and more meaningful bonds. Everything else is *halwa*," Sameena said.

"It will be years before they start to plan long-term and large-scale projects." Shaden said sourly.

"It's fine. They don't need to. The reason Amreen and the Firsts process works is because the connection rejuvenates the desire to take steps for the communal good. They will then start to reduce their stupid, everyday mistakes and become more amenable to ideas that encourage them to think beyond their person."

"Like Erfaan's connections in the city. There are now more and more who ask him fewer questions about why they should spend money and effort on environmental projects. Some of them have been expanding their collaborations to include more departments."

"*Haan.* Or my uncle's food buyers. He *must* be unconsciously nudging them to be better about their general sourcing and practice." Shaden said. This was likely. Saad had been charming and quietly persuasive even before joining the Potohar experiment.

Hamza nodded slowly. On Arfaat's indication, they finally went to devote themselves to the festival.

She felt warm and relaxed in the aftermath of the festivities. This happened every time to the younger members of the community. Latif called it an entanglement high. He theorised that the effects of the shared happiness and camaraderie triggered the same reward centers of the brain as shared intimacy and drugs. Another thing to say goodbye to.

The younger members were okay with this. They found every opportunity to hang out in large numbers. There were many joys to be had when you pushed past these post-modern limits of so-called *personhood*. As persons of the Potohar collective, they were *both* themselves *and* their community. More tightly knit than possible as decreed by the usual definitions of society.

They were packing their supplies onto their bikes. Sakesar's rugged peaks loomed behind them, its shadows slowly dissolving with the dawn light.

The students looked at each other.

Shaden straightened her back and put on her goggles.

"Let's go happen to other people."

Author Statement, Saher Hasnain

Let Us Begin examines how people have discovered how to develop a visceral awareness of others in a way that nurtures the collective consciousness of a community. It demonstrates how even a fledgling 'entanglement' can enhance the human experience and push our boundaries of what personhood entails.

Nest 4 by © Annerose Georgeson, annerosegeorgeson.com

THE LEGEND OF THE COSMOS MARINERS

by Kelli Rose Pearson

"Have you heard the legend of the Cosmos Mariners, my children?" A tiny, ancient woman poked at the fire.

Sparks flitted and floated.

Up!

Up!

Up!

Until they were lost in the starry night.

Zella, Fiona, and Sebastian, the littlest cousins in the Seymour-Hoshi Clan, shook their heads, watching the woman closely. The firelight danced over their faces, which were smeared with dirt and sticky with the remnants of roasted marshmallows. Arlo, who had just turned twelve and was several years older than the others, sat to one side. He frowned, flipped his bangs out of his eyes, and looked away.

"Tell us! Tell us!" Fiona clapped her hands and bounced eagerly.

Zella and Fiona were huddled together beneath a blanket on a log. They were both seven and wore matching blue flannel shirts. They could have been twins but for their hair – Zella's floated like a fiery orange cloud around her head while Fiona's was black and slippery straight down her back. Sebastian, Fiona's older brother by a year and three months, was crouched close to the fire, poking it with a stick.

"Wellllll…" The old woman, known to the children as Aunt Bloom, cocked her head and looked them over with her one small, sharp black eye. Just on the other side of her nose, where you would normally expect to find another eye, was a dark empty socket. Her face was cracked and whorled like the bark of a gnarled desert tree. The children tried not to look at the empty eye too closely, partly out of politeness, but mostly because it made them uneasy – like if they looked at it, they wouldn't be able to look away.

"Pleeeease!" Zella flashed a lopsided smile and batted her eyelashes.

Aunt Bloom paused and turned away from the fire, staring into the velvety shadows of the forest. "Are they ready, the dears?" She seemed to address the darkness politely, as if consulting a wise old friend. "Well, it's about time… gotta know sometime… a lot of potential in this lovey lot." She clenched her wiry weathered hands into fists. "But are their hearts big enough? Bright enough?"

As if in answer, an eerie call drifted through the thick night air from somewhere deep in the woods. "Hoohahooooooooooooo!"

With a whoosh, Aunt Bloom twirled back around. The black pupil of her good eye flickered with firelight.

"Are you children worthy and brave?" She shouted, wagging her finger wildly. "Or will the darkness swallow you up… and *spit out your bones?*"

The children jumped, and then smiled uncertainly. Time spent with Aunt Bloom was never boring.

Arlo narrowed his eyes and his lips twitched into a sulky smile. He leaned toward Sebastian and whispered in his ear, "Maybe Aunt Bloom's finally lost her marbles. Maybe she'll just wander off in the night and disappear from our lives."

"Don't be so mean, Arlo," Sebastian hissed, showing off the gap between his front teeth.

Arlo crossed his eyes and made a face. *If my* parents *weren't so mean, I wouldn't be stuck with these dorks,* he thought.

At that very moment, he was missing his best friend's sleepover, where his whole gang was playing video games and reading comic books. He could imagine the laughter and almost taste the salty sweet of popcorn and candy.

It was such a very little stink bomb, Arlo thought. He felt a giggle tickle his lips. But the scowl quickly returned. As punishment, he had been condemned to spend three days stuck in the forest, camping with his little cousins and crazy Aunt Bloom. No phone, no nothing.

A line formed between Arlo's eyebrows.

It's not fair! Grounded! It's my parents' fault anyway – they don't care. They're always off on their Very Important Business. He felt heavy. *Saving the world and all that stupid junk. Like there's any hope of that!*

Arlo's parents worked for an environmental research institute. He didn't understand exactly what they did, but he heard their worried conversations when they thought he wasn't listening. And he heard bits from the news: Heat wave kills one-third of all bats in Australia in two days! Largest forest fire in history! A once in 500-year storm hits three years in a row! Worst period of species die-offs since the dinosaurs disappeared 65 million years ago!

When he was little, this kind of news had terrified him. Once, he'd seen a grim educational video about how the oceans are rising, and afterwards he was haunted by a recurring nightmare for nearly a year. In the dream, he was building an elaborate sand city on a quiet beach. An odd breeze tickled his ear and he looked up. There, towering over him, was a wave the size of a skyscraper. A dreadful, deafening, rushing noise vibrated through his whole body, like the battle cry of an army of hungry ogres. At the very last moment, just as the wave began to crest, a giant great-horned owl swooped silently down from the sky and lifted him into the air with its talons. When he woke up, his sheets were soaked in sweat.

Now he just felt numb. Besides, his life was fine (when he wasn't grounded). Such bad news felt far away.

"Ehhhemmm!" Aunt Bloom interrupted Arlo's thoughts. She patted her hair and smoothed her skirt. "Now then children...I've decided. I believe that you all are indeed ready for the most certainly very true story of the Cosmos Mariners and their nemesis, the *Hungry Ghosts.*" The last words she growled in a loud whisper.

Arlo hunched over and looked down. *Whatever,* he muttered under his breath.

"Yay!" Fiona's sticky face beamed.

Aunt Bloom looked around the fire and waited until she had their complete attention.

"So, where to start?" She tapped her fingers together and looked up at the sky. When she began, her voice was strong and clear. "Alright, let's start with the ship – that's where the story takes place after all. Well, it is a very, very, VERY large sailing ship. In fact, it is so large, that it is the size of..." She threw her arms open wide, seeming to grow bigger in the flickering shadows of the fire. "...the size of an entire planet!"

She paused and eyed the children expectantly.

They exchanged glances, grinned, and began peppering Aunt Bloom with questions: "Which planet? (They're all different sizes you know!)", "How did it fit in the ocean?", "Were the sailors *giant* pirates?" They knew from experience that the more questions they asked, the better the story.

Aunt Bloom grinned back at them.

"The ship," she continued, "was exactly the size of our planet – the incomparable the marvellous and majestic planet Earth. What a coincidence!" She chortled. "And – imagine it! – it was sailing through the vast, stupendously, mind-bogglingly enormous darkness of space."

Eyes bright, the children leaned closer to the fire. Arlo frowned, pulled the hood of his sweatshirt over his head, and continued to examine the ground.

"Don't forget, my dears – the universe is not only stranger than we imagine, it's stranger than we CAN imagine!"

"I can imagine a lot!" Zella said with confidence.

"Yes, you can, my pet." Aunt Bloom ruffled her hair and laughed.

More like a cackle, thought Arlo with a shudder.

Aunt Bloom made Arlo nervous. He had no idea how old she was. Or even how exactly she was related to him, but his parents had always told him to be respectful. "There's more to her than meets the eye," they had said. *Whatever that means.*

He hadn't seen her in a few years and now he didn't get her. When he was little, he used to hang on to every word of her stories. Like the one about how she lost her eye in a sword fight. *Yeah, right!* Like anyone but a baby would believe that. Now he was old enough to know better than to listen to dumb stories of planet-sized sailing ships in space. He realized that that's just what they were – stories! Nothing more. A pack of lies told to distract the kids while the adults did their so-called important stuff.

Aunt Bloom gave Arlo a sweeping look. Then she turned towards the others. "Where were we?"

"A ship the size of a planet!" Fiona shouted, her eyes sparkling.

"Yes, indeed." Aunt Bloom's one eye sparkled back. "Now, what would you say if I told you that this ship was actually ALIVE? Not a ship at all, but a living, feeling something or some*who*...?

"A somewho?" Zella interrupted.

"Not exactly a what, not exactly a who, something in the middle," explained Aunt Bloom. "It needs water to live, and sunshine, and air, and even a bit of love."

Her face softened and her eye was shining. "And, guess what? We are actually part of this living Earth ship! Not separate at all. With every breath we take, we are a part of the vast breath of the whole thing. It's all interconnected."

Aunt Bloom wove her fingers together.

"Everything touches everything in a big, chaotic tangle of tangledness." She paused and looked at them each in turn. "One of the wonderful things about this tangle is that it means that every small act of kindness ripples out and touches everything else." Her hands fluttered through the air as if she were weaving a spell. "Got it?"

Zella, Fiona, and Sebastian all nodded. Arlo picked a bit of dirt off his sneakers.

"Well, my dears, I must tell you that this ship is just spiraling around the universe and no one has any idea where it is going or what it is doing. Maybe somebody knows, or some*when* or some*where* or some*how* knows… but we? Ha! Lots of kooky ideas out there. As far as we humans are concerned, the destination is completely *unknown*!"

Arlo felt his hands clenching. He was fed up. He had meant to keep quiet, but he just couldn't stand it anymore. "That is just so dumb. The story doesn't even make any sense! A tangle of tangledness? And why would a ship just be sailing around randomly?"

Aunt Bloom looked at him thoughtfully. "It's a good question. But I have a question for you, my dear." When she smiled, her white teeth glinted in the firelight. She tilted her head so that the dark empty socket seemed to stare at him, making him feel dizzy and disoriented.

"Hoohahoooooo…" echoed from somewhere in the forest, more loudly than before.

"Whooooooooooo, darling boy, do you think would save you if a giant wave were about to destroy the world? If the Hungry Ghosts – who wail like an army of ogres – were about to devour you and everything you ever cared about?"

Arlo's mouth dropped open and his stomach tightened. Could she read his mind? He had never told anyone about his dream.

Maybe she had just guessed?

Arlo had always been fascinated by owls. He could name twenty species off the top of his head. Two summers ago, he had volunteered at the local wildlife rehabilitation center and had learned how to care for injured owls. At the time, it had been the highlight of his life. But somehow, over the last year, it had faded to a distant memory. Friends and video games became more important.

Aunt Bloom's one eye bored into his, and then she turned back toward the others. She stooped over, leaning heavily on her walking stick, and lowered her chin. The flickering fire cast strange shadows over her face, making her look not quite human.

She turned back to the others. "Listen closely, loves." Her voice was hushed but fierce. "All of it, the whole ship and everything on it is in grave danger."

Suddenly, she cried out and waved her walking stick above her head. The flames leapt higher into the sky. "There is a deep soul-sucking sadness upon the Earth!" The words boomed through the quiet of the forest and the children gasped, their faces clear in the bright light.

Aunt Bloom drew her eyebrows together and opened her one eye so wide that the white showed all around the black of her iris. On the other side of her nose, the empty socket was as black as a black hole and it seemed to suck in both the light from the fire and the darkness of the forest. "The great lifeforce of our beautiful planet, this wonderful sailing ship, is being devoured by the Hungry Ghosts. We don't have much time..."

Zella and Fiona linked arms and squished closer together on their log. Sebastian froze.

Arlo shuddered, and then glared in disapproval. Not that *he* was scared, he told himself. But scaring the little ones before bedtime? He was going to tell his parents.

Zella frowned for a moment, and then leaned forward and whispered, "But what's a Hungry Ghost, Aunt Bloom?"

Aunt Bloom lifted her chin. "Yes, well, let's see." Her tone was suddenly brisk. "A Hungry Ghost is a kind of bloated zombie-like ghoul. Mindlessly hungry, of course. Belly the size of a hundred elephants and mouth the size of a pinhole. And never, ever, *ever* satisfied. They feed on loneliness and despair. As they get stronger, they drive some people mad with greed and desire, and others become numb and dull."

She lowered her head and then continued, a quaver in her voice. "No evil sorcerer, nor enemy action created the Hungry Ghosts. They come...they come from our very selves. From the wastelands of our souls!"

The not-quite human look came back over her. She looked around the fire and fixed on each of them in turn with her one glittering eye. "But thank goodness for the Cosmos Mariners..." There was a long pause.

"Okay..." ventured Sebastian, "but who *are* the Cosmos Mariners?"

"And how do they stop the Hungry Ghosts?" asked Zella.

Like a rainbow after a storm, Aunt Bloom's face burst into a toothy smile. She sighed, gave a little wiggle, and looked up at the starry sky. After a moment, she squared her shoulders and hummed a few notes of what sounded like an ancient sea chanty. And then, abruptly, she opened her mouth wide and launched into song.

"I'm a far wandrin' pirate, I've sailed for so long

So show me true treasure, and I'll sing you a song

Her voice was clear and hauntingly beautiful – it seemed to fill the forest and the sky. Arlo and the others fell into a hushed silence.

When the Cosmos Mariners take to the sea

Your mind'll stretch wide with such sights that you'll see

There's wonder and kindness, and stardust and all

They've all made the pledge, they all hear the call

'Tis feeling the heartbeat of all that we be

'Tis seeing the magic of forest and tree

And laughing with joy, that'll set the world free"

The last note rose up with the sparks from the fire, disappearing into the starry sky. As it faded, the owl called again from somewhere in the forest.

"Hoohahoooooo!"

Arlo was surprised to find himself as mesmerized as the rest. The words were strangely familiar and for some reason he felt tears prick his eyes. He blinked rapidly, pressed his lips tightly together, and let out a muffled "Hmmfff." The others were all staring in wonder at Aunt Bloom.

"In other words," she continued in a no-nonsense voice, "the Cosmos Mariners are people of all kinds who have taken a vow to spread truth and beauty and kindness in the world. They dedicate their lives to this vow, so they say. Well, as best they can. It isn't easy." A gleam came into her eye. "According to legend, it's an ancient secret society..."

"Do you know any *real* Cosmos Mariners?" Sebastian interrupted.

"Were you listening dear? Didn't I just say it was a *secret* society? They don't go telling their secrets to just anyone." Aunt Bloom chuckled. "Oh, and by people," she added, "I don't mean just human people. A tree, for example, can bring truth and beauty and kindness to the world just as well as anybody."

Zella shook her head. "Wait a seconnnd!" She sounded skeptical. "A tree is a person?"

"Can cats be people?" Fiona asked. "Purring is like a super power!"

Aunt Bloom laughed. "Actually, trees are some of the best people! Mustn't forget the trees." Her tone left no room for contradiction. "Cats too," she added with a twinkle. "And dogs! Most dogs are just love covered with fur."

Arlo brushed his hair out of his eyes, crossed his arms, and continued frowning into the fire.

Aunt Bloom sat down on a log and clapped her hands together to get their attention.

"Soooooooo," she said, her voice pitched high like a snooty school teacher.

"Cosmos Mariners. Much more pleasant to talk about than Hungry Ghosts. We'll start with a simple definition. C-O-S-M-O-S." She spelled out the word. "The whole universe and everything. M-A-R-I-N-E-R-S. An old fashioned word for sailors. Cosmos Mariners. People who sail through the universe." Her voice changed to a loud dramatic whisper. "People who feel the waves and the winds of life itself. Like pirates. Good pirates that is."

"Me!" cried Fiona. "I love big waves. Dad and 'Bastian and I went on a boat in the ocean this summer. *I'm* a pirate!"

Sebastian shushed her. "Let her tell the story Fi!"

"Listen, my loves." Aunt Bloom put her hand to her chest. "The Hungry Ghosts are very real and more powerful than ever before. Somehow, they have convinced people that we are living on a cold dead rock drifting through space and that a living being is no different than a robot – that we are biological robots. Expendable. Replaceable. That an air filter is just as good as a tree."

Aunt Bloom snorted and paused for a breath.

"This is nonsense of course. To put it bluntly…Time is running out. Our world is in great peril." With each word her voice grew louder until she was almost shouting. "If nothing is done…we will all surely DIE!"

In the pause that followed, even the forest seemed to be holding its breath.

Arlo gasped. Suddenly, he heard a rushing vibration that sounded like an army of ogres. He closed his eyes and could see a giant wave towering over him. All his fears came flooding back – the storms, the fires, the death of so many animals. He had tried so hard to ignore this feeling. Now he was shaking and his knuckles were white from clenching his hands. *It's just a stupid story, it's just a stupid story.*

The others looked horrified and angry.

Aunt Bloom let out a heavy sigh that seemed to contain all the sighs ever sighed. "We know how to save ourselves, how to stop it. But we hesitate."

"*Why?*" asked Zella, her voice quavering.

They sat frozen in silence for a long moment.

Aunt Bloom shook herself as if shaking off the gloom. "It's scary. We are all scared. Those of us paying attention. But, listen my dears, you can't be brave if you're not scared."

Aunt Bloom's face brightened.

"And don't forget the Cosmos Mariners! This is where they come in. Their radiance and courage ripples through the interconnected tangle of everything – which makes the Hungry Ghosts lose power. They are our hope for the world!"

At this, Zella jumped up from the log again. "But, can *we* be Cosmos Mariners? I mean, really?"

"Hmmmm…" Aunt Bloom pursed her lips. "To become a Cosmos Mariner, you must sail into the unknown. The pain of the world will feel like a knife in your heart."

"We can do it!" Sebastian drew himself up a bit taller.

"It will leave you bloody and bruised," she went on. "This is the price. Not everyone can make it. But if you do, your spirit will know how to soar like a hawk. That is the reward."

Arlo was paying close attention now.

"Now, Cosmos Mariners don't go around bragging about who they are. But here's a hint: When you are with them, you feel more full of life. They care about the fishes in the sea and the insects crawling on the earth and the birds and the bats flying in the air. Kindness dances in their eyes."

Arlo's mind darted to his parents. The other night his father had been talking softly to his mother, and Arlo saw his father's eyes glistening with tears.

"What's going on?" Arlo had demanded, worried that someone had died.

His father had looked up sadly. "It's the Christmas Island Pipistrelle…a tiny, lovely little bat. I studied it at university. It's just been declared extinct." At the time Arlo had been unreasonably angry, and rushed back to his room to play a video game. A bat? His dad was crying over a bat? How stupid was that?

But Arlo had felt sad too. He and his dad had spent many hours learning about bats, watching documentaries and reading books. They had even visited a famous bat cave in Texas—the largest in the world—and watched the 20 million Mexican free-tailed bats flood into the dusky sky like a river. Bats were his father's passion.

Arlo felt a wave of regret. Why had he been so mean about it?

"Okay, so I know they're secret and everything," Zella said. "But then how does anyone even join? Is there like a test or something?"

Aunt Bloom smiled gently at Zella, then turned and fixed Arlo with her eye. "Well, according to the old stories, there are many, many ways. As many ways are there are stars in the sky. But, as far as I've studied it, I think I've figured out some hints about how to start."

She took the stick she was leaning on and tapped on the ground.

"First is a simple *Yes*! Yes to the very idea of the Cosmos Mariners. Sounds easy, but you can't fake it. The *Yes* must be said with the most tender, truest part of you, with the center of your heart."

She drew a heart in the dirt by the fire.

"Second, you've got to learn to see with your heart and mind at the same time. Tricky! When you can do this you'll be able to understand the world from many surprising points of view. What would it be like to flow through the land for a thousand years? To live in a maze beneath the ground? It takes practice to see through the eyes of a river, an ant, or even another person. When you feel dizzy with wonder and with new possibilities, you'll know you've got it."

She drew the shape of an eye around the heart.

"Finally, take action. Do any type of something that brings joy and goodness and truth. Big, small, doesn't matter. Breathe kindness into the world. Sounds simple? Ha!" She snorted. "It is and it isn't."

Then she added rays, as though from a sun, around the image of the eye.

"After that? Well, with a bit of patience and a bit of luck, other Cosmos Mariners will find you and teach you the rest…that's when the real adventure begins." She pointed to the sky. "And you'll be sailing through the stars."

The children looked up in silence.

"Well then, I just happen to know a little game that they say the Cosmos Mariners themselves use to build up their strength and courage. Would you like to give it a try?" Aunt Bloom asked.

Three heads nodded eagerly. Arlo did his best to look uninterested.

"Okay then. Close your eyes," she commanded. "Take a deep breath and imagine that you are standing on the edge of a silvery smooth ocean that goes on as far as you can see, and farther." She gave them time to imagine.

Arlo sighed, but he closed his eyes and followed along.

"Now, look up at the stars shining above you. Feel the heartbeat of the Earth below you. As you breathe, open your arms wide and imagine that you are getting bigger and bigger, stretching out, out, out into the universe." Her voice was hypnotic. "Remember that every molecule, every atom of your whole body was once a part of a star. Got it?"

They all nodded in unison. Even Arlo.

"Now, breathe in." Aunt Bloom inhaled noisily through her nose. "…And dive! The water is warm and you float like a cork. When you look down, when you look up, all you see is stars."

They sat there with their eyes closed. Arlo could hear the *snap crackle hiss* of the fire and the whoosh of wind whispering in the trees. His cheeks were warm and rosy. A distant "Hoohahooooooooooo!" brushed his ear with feathery softness.

As the sound evaporated into the night, Arlo inhaled and exhaled slowly.

His heart felt suddenly heavy, but in a good way, like it was full.

"Okay," Aunt Bloom said gently. "Now, before you have a chance to think about it – what's the first word that comes to your mind?"

"Wowzee," Fiona whispered.

"Stars so bright they will POP you out of your SEAT!" Zella jumped up off the log and then sat back down again.

"Peaceful..." Sebastian said with a smile.

Arlo didn't mean to say anything, but a word slipped out of his mouth.

"Heart!"

His face heated up and he bit his lip. He glanced at the others, but they were staring at Aunt Bloom with rapt attention.

Aunt Bloom clapped like a small child. "You've got it!" She glanced towards the forest. "You see! I knew they had it in them!"

She took a deep breath and smiled.

The fire was almost out. The children seemed lost in thought, their eyes glowing.

Arlo's eyes were especially bright.

"Okay then, I'm off to bed," Aunt Bloom said abruptly. "See you when our side of the ship is facing the sun."

The children all protested.

"Tell us more!" Fiona cried.

"How do the Cosmos Mariners fight the Hungry Ghosts?" Zella asked.

"Is it dangerous?" Sebastian asked. "I'm not afraid."

"Tomorrow, loves. Tomorrow. We have three glorious days out here. Tomorrow we'll walk to the pond and catch salamanders, then we'll eat lunch under the majestic oak tree and I'll tell you more. Patience. In the meantime, dream of stars."

Aunt Bloom gave them each a big hug. When she got to Arlo, she paused and looked at him with a question in her eye. He hesitated and then gave a slight nod. She wrapped him in a big squeeze. As her head came near his ear, she whispered, "Why not say yes? Tonight..."

After the cousins had washed their faces and brushed their teeth, they all paraded off to bed in their shared tent.

As Arlo tried to get comfortable in his sleeping bag another eerie "Hoohahoooooo" drifted through the silence from somewhere deep in the forest. He was wide awake. Even the idea of sleep seemed absurd. He waited until the soft breathing of the others signaled that they were deep asleep. Then, moving like a cat burglar, he worked his way out of his sleeping bag and slowly unzipped the door of the tent.

He slipped out of the tent, and stepped into the night.

There was no moon in the sky. Only endless stars. His breath quickened and he felt a surge of exhilaration.

"Yes..." he whispered.

Without knowing why, he began to run down the wide path that led from their campsite deeper into the forest. His skin tingled. He breathed in the fresh green smell of the humid night air. He could make out the subtle textures of the dark forest shadows. But just as he was gaining speed and confidence, his foot caught on something—a root! He stumbled, sprawling face first in the middle of the path. As he brushed himself off and spat out a bit of dirt and blood, he looked up. There, in the middle of a little clearing, was an enormous spreading oak tree that seemed to glow in the starlight. Fireflies danced and flickered around it like floating embers.

Limping a bit, he walked toward the tree. From its thick and gnarled trunk, its magnificent limbs flowed up, up, up, as if delicately caressing the starry sky. Looking up at the sky and at the tree, Arlo felt the Earth move under his feet and he felt himself spinning through the vastness of space. His heart was pounding. He sat down with a bump and steadied himself against the tree trunk. As he did so he felt a strange surge of energy, like a jolt of electricity passing up from the ground and though his spine.

"Yes…" He whispered, feeling a bit silly. Suddenly, he realized that he desperately wanted the stories of the Cosmos Mariners to be true. He needed something to give him courage.

An urgent "Hoohahoooooo!" filled the quiet of the night.

He lifted his chin and gazed up into the dark tangle of branches. There it was—a black silhouette of an enormous owl, perched at the top of the tree. And then, just to his right, he heard a gurgling chirping sound. He could make out a football-sized, fluffy, white blob. It was a baby owl.

"Hoohahoooooo…" again from above. Arlo felt like he was seeing double. He was himself looking up at the mother, owl but at the same time he was the owl gazing down at a boy. And then he was the baby owl, scared, stunned, and alone.

Arlo's thoughts raced back to his days at the wildlife rehabilitation center. The baby owlet must have fallen from its nest. Arlo knew it couldn't survive on its own.

Maybe it failed its first flight, he thought. *Like I probably would.*

He kneeled down and looked into the innocent creature's eyes. It blinked back at him. His heart began to beat loudly.

He stretched his mind to remember what he had learned about nest-making. First, he felt around and gathered some twigs and leaves. Then he slipped off his shoes and his fluffy woollen socks. He managed to rip the socks with a sharp stick and pull the yarn apart, which he used to secure the nest. Gently, he scooped up the baby owlet. It was so light in the palm of his hand—a warm trembling ball of feathers. He placed the bird snugly into the nest.

"I'm going to take you home, don't worry."

He took off his sweatshirt and tied it around his waist, with the hood in front. Carefully he tucked the nest into the hood and began to climb.

He reached the first branch easily; it curved almost to the ground and was as wide as a sofa. But by the third branch he began to feel dizzy. His palms were slick with sweat. Looking up, he could see the nest, glowing.

"Hoohahoooooo!" came the call.

He squeezed his eyes shut and began to go higher, feeling his way, testing the branches, which became thinner and more slippery the higher he went.

Suddenly—CRACK! The branch under his foot snapped and he slipped. As Arlo fell, he managed to grab hold of another branch, breaking his momentum. He dangled for a long moment, his palms slippery with sweat. Eventually, after he caught his breath, he scrambled onto another branch and checked on the owlet, who looked oddly content. For what might have been seconds or hours, he clung closely to the trunk of the tree, careful with his precious cargo.

"Hoohahoooooo!" The sound woke him out of his trance.

Gradually, he made his way back down the tree, his eyes streaming with tears. He had failed. He didn't have a plan, but he just couldn't leave the baby owl there alone on the ground—it would surely be eaten by a fox or a coyote. He stumbled back to camp, the nest still tucked in his hood, and he walked like a zombie towards the firepit.

"Hello, my dear," came a low voice out of the dark.

Arlo jumped in surprise. There, perched on a log, was Aunt Bloom.

His lip began to quiver. "I...I tried Aunt Bloom, but I can't..."

"Why ever not, dear boy?"

He held out the nest with the baby owl snuggled inside. "I couldn't make it to the top. I wanted to put it back, but I wasn't brave enough."

"Arlo, look at you. You even gave up your socks for the wee bird. You won't succeed right away every time. It's in the trying. This is where the treasure lies. Listen, we can do it together." She got up and held out her hand. "This is our strength."

"Should I grab a flashlight?" he whispered.

She smiled mysteriously and pointed to her empty eye socket. "I know the darkness, my love, it is my friend. It's where dreams grow and live."

They walked back into the shadows of the forest in silence, until they reached the clearing and the oak tree. Aunt Bloom reached out and put her hand on the trunk of the tree.

"You're going to climb up there?" he asked, surprised out of his melancholy for a moment.

"Ha!" Aunt Bloom snorted. "Physical strength and courage do not a Cosmos Mariner make. They don't hurt, of course, but there are plenty of other ways. I'm just saying hello. Showing my respect."

She tapped her forehead with her bony finger.

"Use that noggin and that heart of yours, dear. Feel your feelings and find the power of your dream."

Arlo stood there, under the stars, under the spreading branches of the oak tree, with the baby owl in its nest. Its fragility hit him in the heart like a knife – his worry for the owl felt connected to his worry about everything. Again, he heard the sound of the ogres' army mingled with the wail of the Hungry Ghosts and he could sense an immense wave of fear and destruction poised over his head.

"Hoohahoooooo…" came the call from above.

He took a deep breath and gazed up. With sudden certainty, he took a step forward. He held the baby owl high up above his head, and he called up into the tree.

"Hello owl! Here is your baby… I just want you to know… well, you are beautiful. Thank you for being alive. I'll stay here all night if I have to, I won't let anything happen to it." He made a little bow, set the baby in the middle of the clearing, and stepped back to the edge of the forest, next to Aunt Bloom.

Aunt Bloom cupped her hands over her mouth and made a sound, just like an owl:

"Hoohahahooooooo!"

They both stood silently and waited.

A dark shape floated up, up, up from the branches of the tree. For a moment it seemed to hover, blocking out the stars. Then, on graceful silent winds, it swooped down and grabbed the little nest in its talons. In the blink of an eye, it disappeared back to its own nest in the top of the tree.

"Hoohahahoooooooooo…"

Arlo's face was wet with tears for the second time that night. Aunt Bloom grabbed his hand and gave it a squeeze.

Without saying a word, they ambled slowly back to the camp. Before he slipped into his tent, Aunt Bloom pressed something flat and round into his hand. It was attached to a string. In the dark he couldn't make out what it was, but he held it tightly in his hand as he fell asleep.

The tent was glowing with morning light when Arlo finally opened his eyes. He felt strangely peaceful. *What a crazy dream,* he thought, blinking with wonder. He could remember every detail. And then he felt it. There, still clenched in his hand, was something flat and round. He was suddenly wide awake. He held the object up to his face and saw, etched in copper, an image of an owl in an oak tree. Slowly, in a daze, he turned it over and on the other side was an eye with a pupil the shape of a heart, surrounded by sunbeams – the symbol Aunt Bloom had drawn in the dirt by the fire.

It was real. It really happened! He wanted to shout with joy. His chest expanded and he felt a warm tingly happiness spread all through his body. He scrambled out of the tent.

As Arlo walked toward the fire to join the others, he found himself humming: *"When the Cosmos Mariners are preparin' for sea, Your mind'll stretch wide with such sights that you'll see…"*

Suddenly he stopped. He remembered where he had heard the song before. When he was a baby, his parents used to sing it to him as he fell asleep. He was sure he had guessed right. *They were Cosmos Mariners!*

At that moment, he heard a rumble on the dirt road. There were his parents, just hopping out of their small electric car.

"Morning Arlo, Aunt Bloom," his dad called out.

"What's for breakfast?" His mom asked with a smile.

They strolled over to the fire.

His mom went on, "We've been thinking, Arlo. We can't force you to love camping. Especially not as a punishment."

"Anyway," his dad added, "you've suffered enough with your boring family. We'll talk later about how you can make up for it. Maybe put in some volunteer time at the wildlife rehabilitation center? For now, if you want to go home and hang out with your friends tonight, that's fine."

Arlo glanced over at Aunt Bloom who was sitting in her chair by the fire, engrossed in her daily crossword puzzle. She looked like any old grandmother. He caught her eye and she blinked it in such a way that he knew it would have been a wink if she had two eyes. His heart felt light.

"Uhhh, maybe Aunt Bloom needs help looking after the others… I was going to teach them some stuff I learned about owls last summer," Arlo said. He wanted to shout, *I know you are Cosmos Mariners. I'm going to be one too!* But then he looked around at his cousins. They needed to find out the truth in their own way—they had to answer the call.

"Such a thoughtful boy," Aunt Bloom said with a sweet smile, nodding her head approvingly. "We do have some small plans to finish up…some matters to explore…some more stories to tell…"

His parents smiled and looked from Aunt Bloom to Arlo with questions in their eyes.

Arlo felt a warm tickling in his belly. The earthy scent of sun-warmed pine needles mingled with the smell of freshly-cooked pancakes. He grinned.

|4|

AUTHOR STATEMENT, KELLI ROSE PEARSON

Quantum social change requires a shift in the fundamental metaphors and myths through which we understand ourselves in relationship to the living systems of our planet. This story speaks to the children in all of us and presents a mythic conceptualization of our role as leaders in the face of ecological destruction.

CONTRIBUTORS

JUDE ANDERSON (AUTHOR)

Jude Anderson's professional career began 25 years ago directing text-based site-specific performance in France when renowned European Festivals commissioned her work. She has worked at all levels of the Australian live art ecosystem and has led practice laboratories and presentations in Belgium, Spain, France, South Africa, Philippines and Australia. Her company Punctum was the sole Australian organization selected for MONS2015-European Capital of Culture international program and is the first ever regionally based company to have won national Green Room Awards. (2017 Experimental category: Innovation in Participation, Excellence in Production). She is an Australia Council 2018 Fellow.

EMMA ARNOLD (ARTIST)

Emma Arnold is an urban/cultural geographer and artist based at the Department of Sociology and Human Geography at the University of Oslo. Her current research is concerned with the aesthetic politics of climate change, approaching this topic through artistic interventions in the city including those connected with the youth climate movement and the actions of environmental activist groups. Emma's art practice includes illustration and painting, street/urban art, and photography. More about her work can be found here: www.emmaarnold.org

TONE BJORDAM (ARTIST)

Norwegian artist Tone Bjordam makes projects related to nature, perception and science. Bjordam works with video, animation films, nature photography, abstract and nature-inspired paintings, intricate, detailed drawings and sculpture installations. She has Masters Degree in Fine Arts from Oslo National Academy of the Arts and her work has been on display in numerous countries around the world. Bjordam is particularly interested in finding ways to communicate science through art, especially the wonder that drives science. www.tonebjordam.com

KRISTIN BJORNERUD (ARTIST)

Kristin Bjornerud was born in Edmonton, Alberta in 1980. She received her MFA from the University of Saskatchewan (2005) and her BFA from the University of Lethbridge (2002). Kristin has received grants from the Canada Council for the Arts, the Saskatchewan Arts Board, the Ontario Arts Council and the Conseil des arts et des lettres du Québec. Her work has been exhibited across Canada and she has participated in artist residencies in Sweden (2010) and Finland (2017). Her work is represented in the collections of the Saskatchewan Arts Board, the Bank of Montreal, the City of Ottawa, and the Canada Council Art Bank. Kristin lives and works in Montréal, Québec. www.kristinbjornerud.com

*Note on collaboration with Erik Jerezano: Brought together by a shared interest in visual storytelling and the value of symbolic language, Kristin Bjornerud and Erik Jerezano have been making collaborative drawings since 2008. Their most recent series *Nosotros Injertáremos* is an investigation of plant life generated from observational drawings, natural history research, memory, and imagination.

AMY BRADY (JUROR)

Amy Brady is the Deputy Publisher of *Guernica* magazine and the Editor in Chief of the Chicago Review of Books, where she writes a monthly column called "Burning Worlds." It explores how contemporary fiction addresses issues of climate change. Her writing has appeared in the Los Angeles Times, the Village Voice, the Dallas Morning News, Pacific Standard, the New Republic, Sierra, Orion, McSweeneys, O, the Oprah magazine, and several other places. She received her PhD in English from the University of Massachusetts Amherst and has won awards from the National Science Foundation, the Bread Loaf Environmental Writers Conference, the Center for Research Libraries, and various academic organizations. She is also the recipient of a CLIR/Mellon Library of Congress Research Fellowship.

DAVID CASS (Artist)

Scottish born artist David Cass has exhibited his multidisciplinary work in a range of exhibition venues and festivals since graduating in 2010. Cass's artistic approach is wide-ranging; each project anchored by sustainability and environmental campaign. While painting and construction are the art-forms he returns to most often, his recent projects also include photography, survey and curation. Bound by their use of found and recycled materials, Cass's artworks each investigate water in some way: from straight depictions of sea, to illustrations of sea-rise. The work featured within this publication is made from thousands of recycled yogurt pots that were molded to form an alternative canvas. Cass recently received Winsor & Newton's top award for his original painting projects, and the Royal Scottish Academy's Benno Schotz prize as the most promising Scottish artist under 35. You can take part in Cass's newest artwork *Where Once the Waters* at davidcass.art/whereonce

ANN EL KHOURY (Co-editor)

Ann El Khoury is an interdisciplinary scholar in Global Studies currently at the University of Technology, Sydney (UTS). She is a life-long fan of science fiction and interested in integrating futures thinking into her work, which has to date primarily been in the area of geographical political economy, global and development studies. She is author of *Globalization Development and Social Justice: A Propositional Political Approach* (Routledge, 2015) and a number of scholarly articles and numerous blog posts. She is currently working on a second research monograph.

DANIELLE EUBANK (Artist)

Danielle Eubank is an award-winning international artist. She has sailed and painted every ocean on the planet in order to help raise awareness about the state of the oceans and climate change. She is a recipient of the Pollock-Krasner Foundation Grant. Danielle Eubank holds a Master of Fine Arts degree from the School of Fine Arts from UCLA. She exhibits widely in The United States, The United Kingdom, as well as in Europe and Asia. She lives and works in Los Angeles. www.danielleeubankart.com

ANNEROSE GEORGESON (Artist)

Annerose Georgeson likes to paint with oil paints and draw with mixed media. Currently she spends time painting and drawing the forest floor. She was born in Switzerland, and came to Canada with her family at age 3. She still lives on the same piece of land where she grew up, near Vanderhoof in the Central Interior of British Columbia. www.annerosegeorgeson.com

SAHER HASNAIN (Author)

A researcher with the Food Systems Group at the University of Oxford's Environmental Change Institute, Saher Hasnain works on various aspects of the global food system. She is interested in global food system transformation, the complexity of human influence in relation to it, and the use of foresight, learning, and teaching to bring about sustainable and systemic change in the food system. Previously, she has worked as an environmental scientist and examined the interconnections of environmental health and urban design. Her professional and personal interests find interesting overlap in works of science-fiction.

ELIN GLÆRUM HAUGLAND (Artist)

Elin Glærum Haugland, b. 1988, Norway, is mainly a painter and also make experimental films and photography. The past five years she has been painting in Norway, Polynesia and the Amazon jungle using mineral and plant color pigments. Using her sensitivity, Elin translates the impressions she receives into an abstract painted language. To her, the painting is alive. Through the encounter with the minerals, nature and her own and other cultures, she is looking for soul and power to give to her works. www.primusprimus.com

JILL HO-YOU (Artist)

Jill Ho-You is an Assistant Professor in Print Media at the University of the Arts in Calgary, Alberta, Canada. Her practice explores the intersection of trauma, embodied memory and the environment through a mixture of print media, installation, bio art and drawing. www.jillhoyou.com

ERIK JEREZANO (ARTIST)

Erik Jerezano was born in Mexico City in 1973. He is a self-taught artist who arrived in Toronto in 2001. Since then, he has exhibited his work in galleries and artist-run centers across Canada, Mexico and Europe. In 2005, he was awarded a Toronto Arts Council Emerging Artist grant, Ontario Arts Council Emerging Artist grant and his work was selected by the Drawing Center viewing program in New York. In 2004, he and two other artists created Z'otz* Collective - another collaborative project that employs drawing, painting, collage, portable sculpture and the written word. He has also been involved in multiple community based mural projects in Mexico City. www.erikjerezano.net

ADELINE JOHNS-PUTRA (JUROR)

Adeline Johns-Putra is Reader in English Literature at the University of Surrey, UK, and was President of the Association for the Study of Literature and Environment, UK and Ireland (ASLE UKI) from 2011 to 2015. Her recent books include *Climate Change and the Contemporary Novel* (Cambridge University Press, 2019), *Climate and Literature* (Cambridge University Press, 2019), and, with Axel Goodbody, *Cli-Fi: A Companion* (Peter Lang, 2018).

REBECCA LAWTON (JUROR)

Rebecca Lawton is an award-winning writer, fluvial geologist, and former Colorado River guide. She received a Fulbright Visiting Research Chair to research her second novel, *49 North*, a view of water crimes in the U.S. and Canada. Her first collection of essays, *Reading Water: Lessons from the River*, was a San Francisco Chronicle Bay Area Bestseller. In her latest book, *The Oasis this Time: Living and Dying with Water in the West* (Torrey House Press, 2019), she "wrestles with the ways that the natural oases of the American West—the underground aquifers that can sustain life in the midst of the most austere deserts—have been sacrificed" (Wall Street Journal). Her climate fiction has been anthologized in Everything Change II (Arizona State University) and Chautauqua. Rebecca now directs PLAYA's residency program for artists and scientists in Summer Lake, Oregon.

OTTER LIEFFE (AUTHOR)

Otter Lieffe is a working class, trans woman and the author of two speculative fiction novels *Margins and Murmurations* and *Conserve and Control*. A grassroots community organiser for over two decades, she has worked and organised around the world with a particular focus on the intersection of gender, queerness and environmental struggles. Since publishing her first novel in 2017, Otter has been building networks to counter the systemic oppressions faced by working-class trans women. In 2018, she helped establish Books Beyond Bars, a trans/queer prisoner support group in the UK. In February, 2019, she founded a new organisation, Trans Feminism International.

JULIA NAIME SÀNCHEZ-HENKEL (AUTHOR)

Julia Naime Sánchez-Henkel is a Ph.D. candidate at the Norwegian University of Life Sciences (NMBU) and a Ph.D. Scholar at CIFOR. Julia holds a bachelor degree in Biology from UNAM (Mexico), in Economics from NYU (USA), and has a master degree in Environmental Economics and Climate Change from LSE (UK). Before starting her Ph.D., Julia was in her home country, Mexico, working at the National Institute of Ecology and Climate Change, where she coordinated and conducted research focusing on deforestation, REDD+, agriculture, and provision of ecosystem services. She has fieldwork experience in Mexico, Peru and Brazil.

KAREN O'BRIEN (CO-EDITOR)

Karen O'Brien is a Professor in the Department of Sociology and Human Geography at the University of Oslo. Her research explores the human and social dimensions of global environmental change, including the relationship between individual and collective change. Her current research project, 'AdaptationCONNECTS,' focuses on the relationship between climate change adaptation and transformations to sustainability, with an emphasis on collaboration, creativity, flexibility and empowerment. She has written and edited numerous books and papers on climate change and its implications for human security and has participated in four IPCC reports. She is the co-founder of cCHANGE (www.cCHANGE.no).

She enjoys reading, writing, running, and yoga, and is curious about all perspectives on change, including the significance of quantum physics for social change.

KELLI ROSE PEARSON (AUTHOR)

Throughout her career, Kelli Rose Pearson has focused on communicating themes of sustainability to wide and diverse audiences. In previous lives, she was the owner of a successful community cafe and events hub in Savannah, Georgia (The Sentient Bean) and a consultant working in the field of regional economic development and sustainability. Currently, she is working towards her PhD on the topic of transformative imagination and leadership for sustainability with the SUSPLACE Marie Curie research network (Wageningen University, NL). Her BA is in Comparative Religion (Carleton College, USA) and MSc is in Environmental Governance (University of Freiburg, DE) reimaginary.com

CHRIS RIEDY (AUTHOR)

Chris Riedy is Professor of Sustainability Governance at the Institute for Sustainable Futures, University of Technology Sydney. He is a transdisciplinary academic who draws on sociological and political theory, futures thinking and transformative science to design, facilitate and evaluate practical experiments in transformative change towards sustainable futures. As a teenager, he dreamed of being a novelist but took a different path into academia, driven by a love for the natural world and a hope to alleviate the suffering he witnessed during international travels. He has published two books, 45 peer-reviewed articles and numerous blog posts. This is his first fictional work.

JORDAN ROSENFELD (CO-EDITOR)

Jordan Rosenfeld is a writer and author of the novels *Women in Red*, *Forged in Grace*, *Night Oracle* and six books on the craft of writing, most recently *How to Write a Page-Turner*, the bestselling *Make a Scene*, *Writing the Intimate Character*, *A Writer's Guide to Persistence*, *Writing Deep Scenes* and *Write Free: Attracting the Creative Life*. Her freelance articles and essays on everything from climate change to the science of awe have been published in hundreds of publications, including: The Atlantic, Mental Floss, New York Magazine, The New York Times, Scientific American, Writer's Digest Magazine, The Washington Post and many more. Jordan lives in Northern California with her husband and young son. jordanrosenfeld.net

NICOLE MARIE SCHAFENACKER (CO-EDITOR)

Nicole Schafenacker is an artist, activist and interdisciplinary arts researcher. She holds a Masters in Interdisciplinary Studies (UNBC) and a BA in Drama (UofA). In 2018 she spent six months living in Bodø, Norway and began to focus her research interdisciplinary approaches to climate change in northern regions. Her most recent project is *Ecologies of Intimacy*, an immersive art installation prompting dialogue on health, social justice and personal relationships to land in northern geographies. Her interdisciplinary artwork has been presented in Canada, the US, and Norway.

SIRI EKKER SVENDSEN (ARTIST)

Siri Ekker Svendsen is a visual artist who lives and works in Oslo, Norway. Her works are primarily concerned with the relationship between nature, perception and consciousness, and the connection between the physical world and the human perception and imagination. She examines this issue through photography and video, with motives of natural phenomena, trees, plants, animals and humans, often in a state of transformation or interaction. Several of her works are based on biology, psychology and mythological material. Siri Ekker Svendsen holds an MFA from Bergen Academy of Art and Design, Norway. Her previous exhibitions include among others Malmö Konstall, Sweden, Grünerløkka Kunsthall, Galleri F15, Preus Fotomuseum, Høstutstillingen, all in Norway, ArtGenda, Hamburg of Center for Contemporary Arts Afghanistan, Kabul. www.siriekker.com

ALBERT VAN WIJNGAARDEN (AUTHOR)

Albert Van Wijngaarden is a young independent scholar from The Netherlands, aiming to learn about the world by living in it. He does this by accepting semester-long visiting lectureship positions around the globe. Although trained as a historian/philosopher, he is currently mainly engaged with questions of humanity's relation to the environment; especially the way people deal differently with responsibilities for—and consequences of—climatic change.

JESSICA WILSON (AUTHOR)

Jessica Wilson is a writer and environmental justice activist based in Cape Town, South Africa. She is deeply committed to social change that is generated through social learning and collective action. Her political advocacy is complemented through regular meditation practice and an exploration of the nature of mind. She has written extensively on climate change, water security, social movements and deep democracy. Jessica holds a BSc in Chemistry (University of Cape Town), a Masters in Urban and Environmental Policy (Tufts University) and a Masters in Creative Writing (University of Cape Town).

CATHERINE SARAH YOUNG (AUTHOR)

Catherine Sarah Young is a Chinese-Filipina interdisciplinary artist, designer, and writer who creates works that investigate nature, our role in nature, and the tensions between nature and technology. Trained in molecular biology, contemporary art, and interaction design, she has various artistic bodies of work, investigating climate change (*The Apocalypse Project*), science and society (*Wild Science*), and sustainability (*Future Rx*). She has an international exhibition, awards, and fellowship profile and works with scientists, industry, and communities, most recently in Berlin, Vienna, Beijing, and the Amazon. She writes science fiction and has been practicing taekwondo for more than twenty years. www.theperceptionalist.com

Acknowledgments

We would like to thank Ann Kristin Schorre and Linda Sygna for their assistance with managing this project; Michelle Fairbanks for the beautiful cover; and Nada Qamber for her creative interior design and formatting. We are also grateful to the University of Oslo and the Research Council of Norway for funding the AdaptationCONNECTS Toppforsk project (250434 /F10). CONNECTS is short for "Combining Old and New kNowledge to Enable Conscious Transformations to Sustainability." *Our Entangled Future: Stories to Empower Quantum Social Change* is part of the Art Connects work package, which explores the potential of narratives to empower collective agency in response to climate change and sustainability challenges.

To participate in this project, we would appreciate it if you could answer a short and anonymous survey that will be used for research purposes: www.surveymonkey.com/r/ourentangledfuture

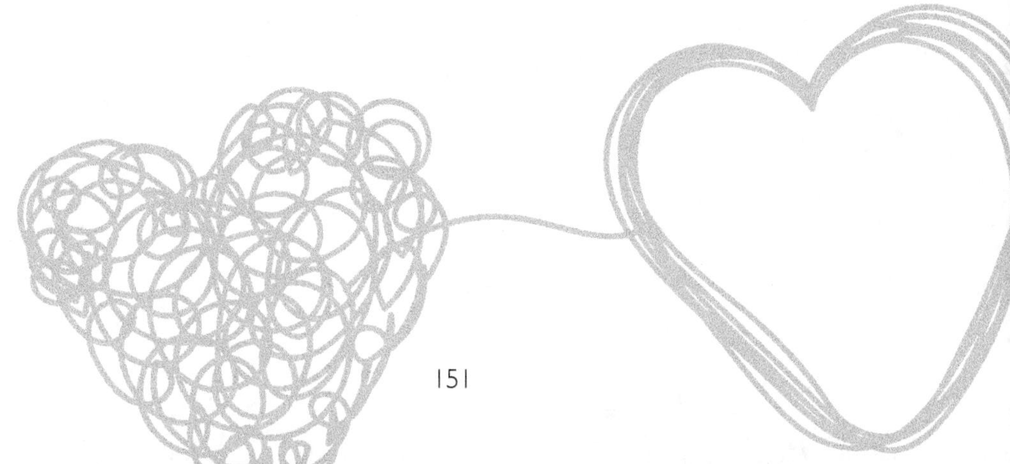